unfriended

rachel vail

PUFFIN BOOKS

PUFFIN BOOKS
An imprint of Penguin Random House LLC
375 Hudson Street
New York, New York 10014

First published in the United States of America by Viking,
an imprint of Penguin Young Readers Group, 2014
Published by Puffin Books, an imprint of Penguin Random House LLC, 2015

THE LIBRARY OF CONGRESS HAS CATALOGED THE VIKING EDITION AS FOLLOWS:
Vail, Rachel.
Unfriended / Rachel Vail.
pages cm
Summary: "When middle-schooler Truly is invited to sit at the Popular Table, she finds herself
caught in a web of lies and misunderstandings, made unescapable by the hyperconnected social
media world"—Provided by publisher.
ISBN: 978-0-670-01307-4 (hardback)
[1. Friendship—Fiction. 2. Popularity—Fiction. 3. Middle schools—Fiction.
4. Schools—Fiction. 5. Social media—Fiction.] I. Title.
PZ7.V1916Un 2014
[Fic]—dc23
2014006247

Puffin Books ISBN 978-0-14-751154-6

Printed in the United States of America

3 5 7 9 10 8 6 4 2

To Amy,
with thanks and love

TRULY

RIGHT BEFORE THE whole thing started with Natasha and the Popular Table, I was standing at my locker with my best friend, Hazel, silently praying that I hadn't forgotten my combination.

I've had this lock since sixth grade, when we got lockers instead of cubbies like in elementary school. My mom took me and my then-best-friend, Natasha, to the store for school supplies the August before middle school started. Natasha and I both chose spinny locks.

My mom thought that the ones with letters that you line up were cuter. At four foot eight, with crooked bangs and lingering baby teeth, the last thing I was looking for was something *cuter*. Natasha was already over five feet and experimenting with lip gloss. And rolling her eyes at stuff I still wanted to play. She was getting a spinner. I wasn't going to get a baby lock while she had a spinny in her basket.

My combination is 14-35-42. All multiples of seven. So

that's easy. Except what if I have a brain fart and think maybe it's multiples of eight? Even if I remember it's multiples of seven, it could just as easily be 7-21-28.

"You should just get a word one," Hazel said, beside me in the eighth-grade hall.

"I can do it," I objected, trying again.

Hazel has a key lock. I think she might be the only one in the whole school. She wears the key on a string around her neck along with her house key and sometimes other random stuff she finds. She has been my absolute best friend since she rescued me in sixth grade, but she is sometimes a lot.

"Just because *those girls* have spinny locks," Hazel said.

"That's not . . ." I said. "I like this kind."

The fact that the popular girls all have spinny locks was not the only reason I kept my spinny lock for this year. For my thirteenth birthday, my parents finally allowed me to get a cell phone, and to sign on to a few social media things—Facebook, Instagram, Snapchat, those types of things. And for every one of them, I set my secret password as locker143542. I know you're supposed to have different passwords for everything, but please.

After my thirteenth birthday party Hazel slept over. We wrote down our secret passwords for everything on sticky notes in case we forget them somehow. Hazel's password is clam0rous, which is turns out does not mean *like a clam*. We both wrote down both passwords, mine and hers, and decided to hide them in our little ballerina jewelry boxes. We have the same ones, we had discovered in sixth grade. The first time she came over and saw mine, we laughed about the coincidence. So corny—the kind with a little ballerina that twirls around when you open it. So girly and cliché, we both thought. As if every little girl is supposed to dream of becoming a tiny ballerina? And collect jewels to fill the box?

Though when I was little I loved that thing. I thought it was so grown-up. But I did see Hazel's point as soon as she made it. I agreed right away it was horribly antifeminist and also tacky. We decided not to throw them away, though. I was relieved, because I really didn't want to throw mine away. But I had just recently been dumped by Natasha for being too babyish. I didn't want my only new-friend prospect to know how babyish I was, deep down. Luckily Hazel agreed the jewelry boxes would be good secret keepers, because what robber would look in a baby jewelry box? She said I was so hilariously ironic.

I looked up the word *ironic* after she left that afternoon.

"A word lock is maybe five dollars," Hazel said, reading my mind as usual. "I could give you the money."

"More like ten," I said. Hazel's parents are not exactly rolling in money anymore. They were, a few years ago, but something happened. She won't talk about it, and I don't want to pry. But she did confide that money is the thing that's keeping her parents from getting a divorce. Their fighting hurts her way more than she wants anybody (except me) to know. So it's not like she was bragging or showing off or anything. I know that. Still. "And the money is not the point. I like this one."

"Uh-huh," she said, twirling her green-tinged hair. "I can see why. It's like a full-on extra-curricular. You want me to try?"

"I got it." I tried again. Click. I yanked the lunky weight of the lock free of the metal loop. "See?"

Someone tapped my right shoulder.

I turned my head to the right, figuring it would be Kim or maybe Jules, one of the girls in orchestra with us. Nobody there. So I turned to my left and saw not Kim or Jules but Natasha.

I had to smile.

She used to tap my opposite shoulder in elementary school and I fell for it Every. Single. Time. We thought it was endlessly hilarious.

Hasn't happened since sixth grade, when she dumped me.

"Still don't know which way to look," she said.

"I'm hopeless." I said. "I never learn."

"Too true," Hazel said. She unhooked my lock from the hole in my locker's handle and held it.

"So, anyway," Natasha said, ignoring Hazel. "You going to lunch?"

"No," Hazel answered. "To the moon."

All eighth graders have lunch fifth, so obviously we were going to lunch. Still. *The moon?* Sometimes when Hazel is trying to sound snide or sarcastic, she just sounds weird.

"Yeah," I said to Natasha. "Sure. How about you?"

"Mmm-hmm," Natasha said. She looked out of the corner of her eye into my locker. I immediately wished it were a little messy, a little less compulsively organized.

"Amazing," Hazel said. "All going to lunch. We have so much in common!"

I gave a small sympathy *ha*, out of compassion. It's awful when you say something intending to be funny and everybody just stands there awkwardly, like you'd announced your pet hermit crab died.

"Hurry up," Natasha said to me. "Dump your stuff. Brooke and I want to talk to you about History Day projects."

"Me?" I asked, still clutching my books.

Natasha smiled, that blinding white smile she's had since her braces came off the summer before seventh. I still don't have enough grown-up molars for my dentist to decide if I need braces, and Natasha's already been done over a year. "Yeah, you."

"Now? At lunch?"

But—I don't sit at their table at lunch. There aren't rules, exactly; like, the principal isn't involved. But everybody knows where you don't get to sit, unless you're invited.

Hazel and I sit at the slightly-nerdy-girl table. We're more social than the kids who only go to the math lab or the library, or those who cut completely. Some of us are on teams or in shows, well, props crew, and most of us are in orchestra. We're well behaved.

The eighth graders who sit at the Popular Table are different. They're practically celebrities. If we had tabloid magazines in middle school, the Popular Table kids would be in

5

all the pictures. *They're just like us! They hand in homework! They whisper secrets!* Although they are *not* just like us. Even girls like Kim and Jules knew when Clay asked Natasha out, and that she dumped him the next week—and we all have theories about what went wrong between them. But nobody at the Popular Table would have one clue who Kim and Jules are, or who I am. Or who we might have a crush on, if anyone. (We don't.) The Popular kids wouldn't be mean to any of us; we just don't show up in their thoughts.

I leaned against the closed locker next to mine. "Brooke? Brooke Armstrong? She wants me to sit with you guys?" I asked Natasha.

"Come on," Natasha said. "Why are you so slow?"

I dropped my books into my locker, making a mess I knew I'd have to come back and straighten up as soon as humanly possible because it would be a pebble in the shoe of my mind until I could get it neat. But I knew it was important to just leave it for that moment and act like it didn't bother me. I grabbed my lunch and swung my locker door shut. Many of the things I'd recently read about popularity emphasized being light and happy, easy to be around.

Hazel still had my lock dangling from her chipped-black-nail-polished index finger, which she was pointing at my chest like a gun.

"Could you . . . ? I'll catch up with you after . . . okay?" I asked her as Natasha and I walked away.

Hazel watched me go without answering. But I could hear my lock slipping into the handle hole behind me, and the trusty, familiar click of it locking tight. I knew I could count on Hazel. She's my best friend. She's prickly and demanding, sure, but she's very loving, down deep. I knew she'd understand. I mean, the Popular Table. You don't get invited to that every day. If she got asked, I'd be happy for her, I think. No, I would. I'd lock her locker for her and wait to hear all about what happened, after. We're solid, me and Hazel.

I didn't even have to look back and make sure.

HAZEL

YOU DIDN'T EVEN look back, Truly.

Just left me standing there like a lawn jockey with your stupid lock dangling from my finger in place of a lantern. No *Come on, Hazel!* Not even a *Sorry, do you mind? I'll be right back.*

Nothing.

All Natasha had to do was show up at our locker area and flash those piano-key teeth at you—and good-bye to me. I might as well have fallen through a trapdoor.

Or never existed at all.

NATASHA

I COULD SEE from across the cafeteria that Brooke thought it was a bad idea, bringing Truly over. Brooke had to be wondering *Why?* Though of course she never asked. She'd just said *sure*, when I suggested maybe I could bring Truly over to our table, this once. *We'll see how it goes,* I suggested, trying to pretend I didn't really care either way, chewing my gum hard to cover the worried warbling in my voice.

Sure, Brooke had answered, shrugging. Like she had nothing to fear, from me or anybody. *Great. Whatever.*

Could she have figured out my plan already?

No. No way.

But I could tell by the way her eyes slid away from my face as I approached our table across the caf with Truly bobbing along beside me that she was annoyed. The way she leaned over and whispered to Clay. And then he turned around to see what was happening. *Hi, Clay. Yeah, remember me? Natasha?*

The girl you kissed and then dumped? By text? Last week?
Jerk.

I have to make sure everybody, I mean everybody, continues to believe I dumped Clay and not the other way around. I have to keep dropping hints about it. My mom is totally right about this, if about pretty much nothing else. Well, she was also right that I have a huge pimple sprouting on my forehead this morning. Yeah, thanks hugely for *that* feedback, Mom. Really started my day off with a boost of confidence. But she is also right that you do *not* want to be known as The Pathetic Girl Who Got Dumped. Even Dad agreed with that, and for him to agree with Mom, well.

I was the hot center of the world while Clay and I were going out. Also right before, when everybody kept telling him to ask me and me to ask him. Right after we broke up, everybody was all over that, too, waiting and watching to see if I was completely sad and devastated. Lulu kept asking if I was "okay." *I'm great,* I told her. *I don't need him. Please. I dumped him!* That's what Dad said I should tell everybody, and it felt good, tough, saying it. The sympathy was nice until it dried up, but still I didn't need people thinking Clay dumped me. This is part of the plan with Truly, to make sure even the losers and nobodies in school have it straight: I dumped *him.* Not the other way around.

But the other part of it is: although Brooke is my best friend, she's also obviously long-term close with Clay. And she acts like she's like practically the president of our group of friends. People think she's so chill and Zen and nice but I honestly think that's all an act and she is just as scheming as the next person. Me, in other words, ha-ha. Everything she says, Evangeline and Lulu are like, yeah, or that's so funny.

They definitely think I'm funny and fun, too. But second always to Brooke. Now that I'm not going out with Clay anymore, I'm practically invisible. Nobody was even noticing me at all. I got a new haircut when I was at my father's apartment last weekend. One day's worth of compliments. One. Truly always complimented my hair, back when.

Beside me, Truly was nattering on. "Why does Brooke want to talk with me? Is it because of what I said in science this morning about buoyancy, and she laughed?"

Yeah, that's the huge subject we love to confide about, Truly: what hilarious thing you said in your science class that I'm not in. Absolutely. It's that freaking fascinating.

I was near ready to stop right there and be like, you know what, Truly? It wasn't Brooke's idea to bring you over, so get over yourself. Stop concocting this little romance you're imagining with her. It's embarrassing. She doesn't even know who you are. She didn't invite you—I did. But now, forget it. Go back to your green-hair freak friend. Buh-bye!

But I hadn't yet had time to confide the story of why I had to dump Clay, who was either a jerk or too boring (must decide which) and maybe when he tried to kiss me he, like, had bad breath or something. Yeah, that's good. Bad breath.

Also, it would be mean, to dump her two minutes after inviting her.

And for my plan to work, I could not be mean. Ever. Nobody could think of me as mean ever again. I had to displace Brooke as the Queen of Nice.

So instead I smiled at Truly and whispered, "Trust me."

BROOKE

NATASHA TRIED TO act casual about bringing that girl Truly over to our table at lunch today. When Natasha tries to act casual, her joints get out of whack, like she's dancing to music by Stravinsky. My older sister Margot does ballet. That Stravinsky stuff is like an ear infection.

So I said, "Sure, whatever, that's great," this morning because Natasha was at risk of dislocating a shoulder, being so violently casual. Also it is fully fine with me if some random kid sits with us at lunch or works with us on the History Day project or whatever. The more the merrier. Natasha gets very dramatic about stuff like that. Maybe it's the not-having-any-siblings thing. Makes her a little shocky I think. Gotta love her, my dad would say.

The girl she brought over, Truly, has gray eyes. That, and the fact that she is very little, almost looks like a sixth grader, was all I really knew about her. She's been in some of my classes but mostly keeps to herself.

Her idea was to do Benedict Arnold as a topic for our History Day project. Cool, I said, and everybody agreed. Then Clay and I went outside. His older brother and mine have been best friends since nursery school, so Clay and I were friends before we were born. They are both very focused people, our brothers. Both are good at school (though his brother was valedictorian) and sports (though my brother was better at that). They left for college last month. But it's different for Clay. He has only the one brother. For me it's just marginally quieter. I mean, my brother Otto is great. I miss him. But there are still three of us kids home. Clay was flat-out lonely.

"When is that even due?" he asked me.

"The History Day thing?"

"The topic, yeah."

"I don't know. Did you lose your assignment pad again?"

"It's in my locker," he said. "Did you see the color of that girl's eyes?"

"Truly?"

"Is that really her name?"

"Her real name is Gabriela, I think—that's what the teachers always say, first day, right?"

"Wonder why they call her Truly then."

"Maybe she always tells the truth," I said. "Is your name really Clay?"

He shoved me. "Shut up."

It's his middle name. Edmund Clay Everett. His brother is James Thomas Everett III, called JT. They're not as formal as that might sound. They have worn-out rugs, wood floors, and a golden retriever named Milo. His dad, James Thomas Everett Jr., (called Mr. Everett) is always looking for his glasses, which are usually on his bald head. He's African American. Clay's mom, who lets us call her Maggie, is white. She wears slippers in the house and no makeup; she always looks like she just got out of the shower and usually has a book dangling from her hand. She runs five miles a day, like Clay, but she does hers before anybody else wakes up.

I once asked Clay's dad if he runs, too. "Not even a fever," Mr. Everett said.

Jack tossed a tennis ball over toward us. Clay one-handed it. Before he tossed it back to Jack, he asked me, "So what do you think I should do?"

"About your lost assignment pad? Or Natasha?"

"Duh."

Just because he'd broken up with her didn't mean he'd stopped thinking about her. I have really good peripheral vision, but a blind man couldn't miss how Clay watches Natasha. Still, though.

I shrugged. "She's telling everybody she broke up with you."

"Fine with me," Clay said. "Makes me sound like less of a jerk."

"So don't do anything, if you don't care."

Clay tossed the ball back to Jack. "She's just always so . . ."

"So . . ." I echoed, smiling at him. I knew what the problem was, and that it had nothing to do with setting the story straight.

"So tell me what to do about her. She's mad at me again."

"Apologize."

"I don't even know what I did."

"Still," I said. "Or maybe don't. Maybe just leave it alone. Do you really want to go back to that? All the drama?"

"No way." He caught the ball again. "She's mad at me and then suddenly she's so not because she's all fluttery and, like, pressing up next to me, and then boom I don't know what I did but she's cursing at me or crying . . ."

"Yup."

"So I should just back away."

"But?" I asked.

He kicked a rock. "But she's so freaking hot."

I had to laugh.

He tossed the ball back to Jack. "You suck."

I held up my hands to Jack.

"Doesn't anything ever piss you off?"

Catching the ball, I thought for a minute. "Mosquito bites."

"Mmm-hmmm," he said.

I tossed it back to Jack. "Humble brags."

"What's that?"

"Humble brags. You know. When people are like oh, I'm so frustrated I only got a ninety-seven on that test, now my average is wrecked."

"Who said that, Akron?"

"This morning," I said. "It was classic,"

"He said a ninety-seven wrecked his average?"

"He said it was because he hadn't eaten a good breakfast."

"No."

"It was a thing of beauty."

"See?" Clay poked me in the shoulder. "You even love the stuff you hate. How do you do that? Nothing bugs you. It's just weird."

I shrugged. No use letting stuff bother you that you can't do anything about. And some things, you can't do anything about. Like who your best friend likes. Or doesn't.

"Nothing bothers you either," I pointed out.

"Untrue! I'm constantly hungry," Clay said. He started counting on his long fingers. "People who walk too slow in the halls. Seams in socks. Anybody being mad at me. Shin splints. Pudding. Are you kidding? Everything bothers me."

"Speaking of which . . ."

Natasha was on her way out, walking toward us with Theo and Lulu and Evangeline and all those guys.

Clay turned back toward Jack, held up his hands for the ball. "That girl Truly's pretty cute though, too."

I laughed. "You're so doomed."

"Yeah."

He smiled his twinkly-eyed sad smile and a weird urge hit me: to throw my arms around him and hug him tight. That exact urge has been popping up more often lately, and it pisses me off. See? That's something. But it's the one I'd never tell him. We're friends, me and Clay; it would be way too awkward to admit I maybe *like him* like him. Obviously he doesn't feel that way about me. I just have to wait the urge out, like a cramp. Walk it off.

"Still too quiet in your house?" I asked him instead of continuing the topic of which girl he should go for. Because, yeah.

"Way too quiet," he said softly.

Ugh. I'm so not willing to be like every other girl in our grade, following after him, sighing. So I shook my head and turned away, just saying, "Yeah?"

"Yeah." He followed after me, talking right next to my hair. "My parents actually said last night, 'Now that JT is gone, you'll get a lot more of our attention.'"

"Oh, no," I had to say, because that was like his worst nightmare.

"Right?" Clay asked. "So, yeah. Fully doomed on basically every level."

Preach.

CLAY

TO DO:

1. Focus on schoolwork
2. Stay AWAY from Natasha
3. Topic for History Day project (due WHEN?)
4. Find assignment pad (somewhere under the mess in my room? In locker?)
5. Take a shower/use deodorant. Yuck. The whole getting wet/getting dry cycle. And goo in my pits? Maybe skip this one.
6. Find a new series to binge on. Maybe ask Jack what he's watching these days.
7. NO! No more TV/Internet/Facebook until ALL homework is done. BE A TOOL like JT. Making a to-do list is a total tool move. On my way, yo!
8. Clean room/surprise Mom and Dad? Or will they be pissed I'm not studying? Probably.

Never mind that one either, then. Crossing stuff off this list like a BOSS.

9. Ask Brooke if I should respond to the billion Snapchats from Natasha.

10. Text JT again: possible to Skype soon? (Whenever. He's busy. Being a tool.) Maybe find something funny on the Internet to send him. #research

11. Friend that girl Truly.

12. Or maybe not?

13. ??? ugh so bored nothing to do.

TRULY

MY BEST FRIEND, Hazel, stood over my desk first period today with a note dangling from her fingers. I had tried to talk with her after lunch yesterday, but she walked away fast. I told myself maybe she was rushing to class. I left her chat and text messages last night, just to make sure everything was still normal between us. But she ignored me until the end of first period today.

"Hi, Hazel!" I said. She didn't answer. The note was folded up tight and small, my name in her tiny, neat green script on the outside. I watched it drop onto my desk. Hazel left math without me, her green hair bouncing behind her.

The note said she hated me because I only thought about myself, was spoiled and a bully and mean.

I sat at my desk for a few minutes and just read it over and over.

Out in the hall, I showed it to some of our other friends to see what they thought. Esther Luo said that Hazel's grandma had broken her hip last night. But everybody else was like, that's not a good excuse. What does her grandmother's broken hip have to do with saying all those mean things about Truly?

Of course we all knew what Esther meant, that Hazel was just upset about her grandma so she was striking out at me. Esther is a very understanding person, very kind. But she was making excuses for Hazel. Everybody agreed.

"Not excuses," Esther protested. "Just a possible explanation. I think she went up the C stairwell."

"No way," we all said. But none of us went up there to see, because you could get suspended for going up the C stairwell. There are rumors people go up there to make out or do drugs. There's supposedly a locked closet for custodial supplies or maybe access to the roof up there. We stood looking up it for a minute but didn't hear anything, so we decided to get going to second period quick so we wouldn't be late. It seemed unlikely even Hazel would hazard going up the C stairwell.

When I got to English, I guess I was looking pretty wrecked. Natasha came straight over to me and whispered with her face all sad and concerned, "What happened? What's wrong? Tell me!"

So I showed her the note Hazel had dropped on my desk. As she read it, her perfectly pink-glossed mouth opened wide in disbelief. "Oh, my gosh," she whispered. "That is *so* mean." She pulled me into a hug and didn't let go until the teacher, Ms. Fenton, said to take our seats please.

My mom had said to be careful, last night, when I told her about being asked to sit at the Popular Table yesterday. I think she worries that popular girls are all secretly mean. I explained that the girls who sit at the Popular Table are actually the nicest girls in the whole eighth grade. Things were probably different when Mom was my age and it was called junior high school. I've seen some of those movies—it's awful, and I don't just mean the hair.

Natasha passed me a note when Ms. Fenton turned to write the homework on the board. In her still-so-familiar plain blue print, it said, "Are you okay?"

"I guess so—just really confused," I wrote back. Girls from the Popular Table love stuff like that, passing notes and somebody who's been wronged.

On the way out of English, Natasha said, "See you later, Truly!" For almost two years, most of sixth and all of seventh grade, plus the first few weeks of eighth, she had barely glanced in my direction. I tucked her note into my pocket, too.

Hazel ignored me the whole rest of the day, walked away every time I got near her. I didn't want to assume I was invited to sit at the Popular Table again, but I also didn't want to sit next to Hazel at our regular table either, after that note and the ignoring. So I was planning to volunteer in the library at lunch. I wasn't very hungry anyway. But Natasha hooked her arm through mine before lunch and chatted with me the whole way down to the cafeteria and sat down with me right there at the Popular Table like that was my normal spot.

23

Those kids laugh a lot. At my regular table—I hadn't noticed this before but we kind of pick on one another. "That's so stupid," Kim will say if Jules says something is cute, or Hazel will go, "You know that makes no sense at all," if Kim comes up with some theory. I'm sure I do it, too. It's just our sense of humor, I've told myself. Only Esther says, "That's an interesting point," even when it isn't.

I didn't talk while I sat at the Popular Table today. I smiled and listened, watching closely. Lulu giggles at everything. Evangeline disagrees and acts tough but I think is just kidding. They talk very fast, all laugh in bursts, and clearly all watch the same TV shows. I will have to binge-watch tonight, in case I'm invited back again. Mom will understand and probably let me watch more than I'm usually allowed.

When Lulu's mom died a few years ago, my mom helped organize people to bring over food and stuff to her family, even though we didn't really know the family well. She used to ask me sometimes how Lulu is doing, but I have never really known, other than she seems great, very smiley. And of course Evangeline is famous for being so awesome at both sports and school that even the parents know her. And then there's Brooke. Her whole family is cool. There are four kids, and each one is the most popular in whichever grade. They own a bookstore and all go bike riding together, looking like a commercial for something awesome and expensive when you see them flying by, all gorgeous, laughing together. They're the family all of us wish we could be in.

"What's she like?" Mom asked last night.

"She's . . . really nice," I said. "She seems . . . happy."

"Nice," Mom said. "That is such a good quality to have, just being happy."

"Yeah," I said.

She's especially cautious about Natasha, probably because of our history. I cried a lot in sixth grade. But maybe also because of her own history with Natasha's mom. They were best friends until Natasha's mom took me to get my ears pierced for my tenth birthday, even though my mom had told her not to. Mom made me take the earrings out and let the holes close. I still have the studs in my jewelry box. I'll never throw them out because that day was one of the happiest of my life, until I got home. Mom made me wait until this year, when I turned thirteen. She said it was "unconscionable" for Natasha's mom to take me. I get that, but I think Natasha's mom was just trying to be nice. She's one of those moms who wants to hang with the kids and be like a friend to us. She's a little scary to me sometimes with her long nails and too much eye shadow and cigarette breath, but then sometimes I think she seems lonely and a little, like, trying too hard to seem upbeat.

Mom says her worries about Natasha befriending me again have nothing to do with her own history with Natasha's mom; they grew apart, as happens sometimes with friends. It's that Natasha is edgy. And though edgy is sometimes very attractive, it can sting. Mom's just protective of me. She can't help that.

I rolled my eyes the way Natasha does at that, to show

Mom I'm too grown-up for that kind of protection. And maybe a little edgy myself. But I know in truth I'm lucky I can talk honestly with my mom about what's going on socially at school. Most kids can't do that with their moms.

When I got home today, I told Mom about the latest with Hazel. I showed her the note. We sat at the kitchen counter together, drinking seltzer from our new seltzer maker. I love when I get special time with her, even though my brother and sister need her more.

Mom thought it was very inappropriate, all those things Hazel had said about me. Even if her grandmother's hip was broken, and she felt left out when I sat at a different lunch table. "And why is it written in green ink?" Mom asked.

"Hazel always writes in green ink," I explained. "It's her *thing*."

Mom raised her eyebrows for a millisecond. She says she loves Hazel but I'm not sure that's true. I know Hazel's moodiness and rudeness sometimes bother Mom. I think the green ink bothered her, too. I'm not sure why it would. But I'm pretty sure it did.

"Do you think I should call her?" I asked Mom. "Or Skype or e-mail or . . ."

"Sure," Mom answered. "Whichever feels most comfortable to you."

"What should I say?"

We brainstormed a couple of possible openings but finally agreed I should just say exactly what I felt, which was that I was surprised and confused by her note, and then let Hazel say what she needed to say. Maybe she would say she was sorry, she was just in a bad mood. Maybe she'd blame her grandmother's hip. Or maybe she would say that she was mad about the lunch thing.

I wasn't sure what to say about that, if that's what she said. I mean, I could say I was sorry, but that wasn't really true. I was, truthfully, happy I got asked to sit at the Popular Table. I could say I was sorry she was hurt that I got asked to sit there and she didn't, which is true, but there's really no way to say that without sounding like a complete jerk. The nonapology apology is just the worst.

So that's why I was nervous about making the call. I'm not confident Mom fully understood that part, which made me feel strangely lonely.

I went up to my room to plan it out independently a little. Maybe I should just tell Hazel that I knew she was upset I'd gone off with Natasha and those guys, and apologize, and promise not to sit with them anymore.

But that felt really terrible. Is that the only way to handle it and still be a truly good person? My parents started calling me Truly when I was like two years old, because I was always so earnest, they said, always trying do the right thing and seeming so mature. Truly Yours, they called me for a long time, until it got shortened to just Truly. I don't want to let them down, or myself either. Be called Untruly. But what was the right thing to do? Dump my new friends for my best friend, even if she was the one being meanest to me? Should I take it, though, because maybe she's just feeling hurt and it's my fault? I was asking myself these hard questions, lying on my bed with my stuffed dog Francisco pressed over my face. Why can't I be friends with everybody and also not have anybody be mad at me?

Why does Hazel make me feel like I'm so evil, just for getting to be slightly friendly with some nice kids in our grade? Is that fair?

I was starting to get a little mad back at Hazel. She says I am spoiled a lot, mostly whenever she is in a fight with her mother, but she has never said any of those other mean things to me before this, or put it in writing.

I sat up and reread my two notes from today. Maybe I shouldn't be as quick as usual to say *That's okay don't worry about it* if Hazel does apologize right away. I decided I would just listen to whatever she said and maybe write down her words on my pad and then just say, "Okay, I'll talk with you more about this tomorrow. Bye."

She didn't pick up the phone—her cell or the family's phone. She's not big on answering either because she is phone-o-phobic, or so she says. I don't know if that is a real thing. My brother and sister both have learning challenges that neurotypical people don't always understand, though. Older relatives think my brother and sister should just "try harder" or "stop acting like that" which is both mean and clueless—so I'm extra careful not to question people about their issues. Anyway, I was kind of relieved that she didn't answer.

After dinner, before I went to bed, I checked my computer. Hazel hadn't e-mailed me, but Natasha did. *See you tomorrow . . . meet up at the wall?*

The wall is where all the kids who sit at the Popular Table "chill" before school.

HAZEL

BEFORE TRULY FLOUNCED off to lunch with *those people*, she said, "I'm sorry if you're feeling hurt. I didn't intend to hurt you, Hazel. I really didn't. You're my best friend and I don't want you to be mad at me. Okay? Talk to me. Please? Okay. Or don't. I'm here whenever you want to. Just . . . I . . . okay."

I stood there, stunned, beyond words. Then I climbed the forbidden steps in C stairwell up to the pee-smelling landing, my new hideout because none of the zombie-automatons in this horrid school dare go where the rules say don't, and wrote her a new note, which I will probably never deliver because the first one obviously backfired but still.

Truly, (not Dear)

Let me outline what is wrong with your hideously self-serving nonapology:

A. There's no IF. Obviously I AM hurt.

B. You're only sorry if (hahahaha, if? No, clearly I am, so: that) I am hurt. When you should be sorry for the way you acted. You're sorry I'm hurt because that complicates your life. Sorry like you wish I would just deal with the fact that you are completely dumping me for a better (not really better, just more Popular) deal. You're sorry that you have to deal with my feelings, after we've been best friends all this time and bam, you unfriend me in one cold heartbeat. Just the way Natasha did to you, btw. Remember that? And who was there for you, back then? Yeah, that's right; it was ME.

C. How about being sorry for what YOU DID instead?

D. Whether you *intended* to hurt me or not (which is debatable. Also, irrelevant), you did hurt me. You dumped me, hard, and publicly, and so coldly I still have icicles in my hair. I might dye it blue, to match the icicles.

E. How many times have we talked about nonapology apologies and how horrible they are?

F. I'm your best friend? Really? Wow. I mean, I thought I was, but—how can I be if you feel no qualms about just abandoning and humiliating me like that? That's how you treat your best friend? Think about that for a minute.

G. I'm sure you don't want me to be mad at you. You probably want me to just disappear, or maybe encourage you, or envy you. Just not be mad at you. But tough.

H. You're here for me? Ha! Sure. Unless the Popular Table whispers your name. Then adios to me, you're gone. Without a glance back.

I. Good-bye, Truly. I don't know who you think you are, Miss Popularity or Miss Social Climber or what, but it's not the person I thought you were: smart, funny, deep,

and kind. You're dumbing yourself down
and trading your soul for their attention.
Someday, mark my words, you'll regret this.
And it will be too late when you figure out
who your true friends were.

J. Watch out for Natasha especially.

NATASHA

THE WHOLE *TRAGEDY* with Truly's freak friend Hazel is soooo brain-crushinglyyyyy dulllllll. Nobody wants to hear it anymore HELLO! But Truly just keeps playing that crap up for all it's worth. Brooke is such a sucker for everybody else's problems, always listening, that whole *oh I care so much* bull. Just to make everybody like her. Well, I can do that, too, tilt my head and act like Truly's trauma is so very fascinating. I was soooo sympathetic these past few days. *Oh, no, Truly—are you okay? I can't believe Hazel wrote a nasty note to you! That's (still) terrible!*

I was nauseating myself.

But whatever, I can take it. By the end of today, Truly was walking with me to my classes, nodding at everything I said, laughing exactly right at my jokes, asking my advice.

In elementary school, Truly gave *me* the advice. She always chose what we'd play, helped me with my homework, comforted me when my parents were harsh. Now it's me comforting her, getting to be the superior one for once. *Oh, that's awful! Hazel really said that? Totally not okay!*

So she ought to remember how good a friend I am to her and not sit between Clay and Brooke. Or does she not even realize that as fast as I brought her in I could make her disappear? And Brooke would not care or even fully notice. Same with Clay.

If Truly can't figure this fact out on her own, I am going to have to explain a few things to her.

Nicely, of course.

Because I am so unbelievably nice.

9

BROOKE

MY SISTER MARGOT and I sat together on her bed, the top bunk.

"Will you have to drop ballet classes?" I asked her.

"Hope not," she said.

Wow. Okay. I was kind of kidding. "What do you think will happen?"

Margot shrugged in that Margot way. It looks so graceful and world-weary.

"Well, they'll get money from selling the store, right?" I asked.

"Yeah, some," she whispered, stretching out her long string bean self into a straight line along the bed. She pointed her toes hard, then lifted her legs in a straight line up toward the ceiling. She extended her arms past her ears, so her long fingers tickled the headboard. I've fallen asleep hearing these stretches above me forever. "But after they pay off all their debts, how much will be left?"

I stretched out beside her, my jock body heavier, thicker, less bendy. But my feet, unlike hers, could flatten against the ceiling. Good calf stretch.

"You should come up with a talent," Margot suggested. "You don't get college scholarships for popularity, and no way they'll be able to pay."

"Ugh," I said. "College. That's a million years away."

"It's not," Margot whispered, smooth and nearly silent. "Wake up. And especially with Corey's therapy, there's not likely to be a lot left over for you."

"I know," I whispered back. Still. Eighth grade. I have forever. I do.

We listened to the *thunk* of the basketball against the hoop in the driveway, Dad out there working with Corey. He'll have more time at home now, once the store gets sold. Mom, too. And something else will turn up. They're hardworking. Good people find a way. That's what they'd said, after they broke the news to us this afternoon about selling the store. We'll have to hold off on some extras for a while, but we'll find work and pull through. We've got each other. We're the richest people in town that way. We'll be all right.

My phone buzzed in my pocket. It was Clay, asking how I did on the math test and if my parents would be mad. Yeah, like they'd care about my math test at this point. Way bigger fish to fry. But I just said, *they never ask*.

"You still in love with Clay?" Margot asked after I'd gone back and forth texting him a few times.

"No," I lied. "You still in love with JT?"

37

"No," she lied.

"Cool," I said as phone buzzed again. "So we're all good."

"Absolutely."

We lay there beside each other until dinner not talking, our bodies parallel, our feet on the ceiling.

CLAY

MY BROTHER JT got an 800 on his math SATs and a 5 on his calculus AP test. Those are the best scores you can get. He graduated first in his class. He won multiple awards at graduation, was editor in chief of the school paper, and played varsity soccer. He got into his first choice of college early.

Everybody is impressed with him. Including me. He's my favorite person, which doesn't make me unique. Girls all want to go out with him, and probably some guys do, too. He's the nicest guy I know. He volunteered at the soup kitchen every Sunday morning all through high school with Dad. He has inside jokes with pretty much everybody, including some of the soup kitchen regulars. Also teachers.

So how do I break it to my parents that I just got a 78 on my math test?

I know they think I'm not as smart and not as hardwork-ing as JT. They're totally justified; it's the truth. I'm not. JT doesn't get distracted by reading the entire Internet or playing Xbox for hours at a time or texting with a girl who is not his girlfriend and never will be because she's his best friend. Well, first of all because his best friend is a guy. A guy who is my best friend's older brother. And they wouldn't text each other more than, like, *Want to go get some pizza? Sure meet you in 10.*

Not like me and Brooke. We can go on texting each other for an hour or more at a time. She got an 89 on the math test. And her parents are completely chill about grades, so 89 is fine.

I don't even know if mine are chill about grades or aren't. They have been until now, but I always got A's and anyway they were focused on JT. Nobody ever brought home a 78 around here before.

What if they punish me?

What if they say, *Maybe if you spent a little more time focusing on your schoolwork and a little less time socializing . . .*

Or what if they don't? What if they're just like, *Oh, well, that's fine. Maybe you're just a C student and that's all we can expect from you.*

What if they're actually proud of a 78, from me?

I shut my computer and turned off my phone. The test paper's big scrawled red 78 glared at me. I slipped it under the textbook, which I opened up to chapter four, determined to cram some of this stuff into my brain. I was good at math last year and every year before this. No reason I should suddenly fail it now. I just have to buckle down, maybe do the homework.

After about five minutes of staring at the page without registering anything, I shut the textbook and opened my computer. There have to be like video tutorials online to help you make sense out of solving quadratic equations. What the heck even is a quadratic equation?

When I looked up, more than an hour had passed and Dad was calling me down for dinner. I hadn't learned any math but I had seen a bunch of hilarious cat videos.

I dashed down the stairs. As I was putting out the plates and silverware, Mom and Dad were doing their final stirs of the stuff on the stove and discussing current events. Dad said something about Syria. Mom made a point that included the words *economics of the region*. Dad agreed.

Mom popped open a bottle of wine and poured two glasses, which she carried over to the table. Dad brought the steaming bowl of pasta with some sauce on it that smelled amazing.

I love to eat. I get happy just picking up a fork.

We sat at the table, with its lost-tooth gap where JT should've been. They kept talking about Syria or the economy or whatever it was they were discussing. I ate. It was delicious.

"How was school today?" Dad asked. They both held their forks in midair and looked at me.

"Okay," I said, moving my eyes from one to the other. "What?"

"How are your classes going?" Mom asked. Fork still at half-mast.

I looked over at the seat where JT wasn't and wished for him to materialize. No luck.

"You liking English?" she asked, lowering her fork, still holding its pile of pasta, to her plate.

"Yeah. Ms. Fenton is great," I said. "Really sarcastic and funny."

"And how about math?" Dad asked. He made a big thing of refolding his napkin on his lap. Fine. I plopped my napkin onto my lap, too. "Math going well this year?"

"I don't love Ms. Davidson, honestly."

"Okay," Dad said. "But how are you doing in the class?"

Usually JT would be the one talking about his classes and I'd be free to just eat in peace or maybe mock him. Or, like, fall out of my chair.

"Okay, I guess," I said. I choked a little on a hunk of bread. I like to just eat while I'm eating.

"It's interesting—we ask you about your classes and you tell us your feelings about the teachers," Dad said.

I took some more bread and loaded it up with butter.

"I loved algebra," Mom said.

"I think my favorite thing about algebra is the definition," Dad said.

"What definition?" Mom asked.

Dad rubbed his forehead where the hair isn't anymore, the way he does when he gets excited about a topic. His glasses, as always, toppled off. "The word *algebra* means the reunion of broken parts."

"Really?" Mom asked. "That's so interesting. Don't you think, Clay?"

"Yeah," I said. "Sure."

Dad smiled at me. "It comes from the Arabic words for *reunion* . . ."

"And *of broken parts*?" I asked. "Just a guess."

They both nodded and smiled, waiting for me to say more, like JT would have if he were here instead of me. Maybe quote from some famous mathematician or make a reference to Syria.

"Cool," I said. I ate some more pasta. They waited patiently. "This is delicious," I said.

"Oh, good," Mom said.

"What else is going on in school?" Dad asked, like he knew something was up, something was going wrong. Maybe they send home an e-mail or something if you get a bad mark and this was their way of interrogating me.

"Nothing," I said. Tough. Too bad. So they didn't win the lottery twice. Great. I'm stupid. Fine. What? I'm not JT? Right. I'm not.

Sorry.

Nothing I can do. Ask me directly or leave me alone. A 78 is not the world's worst tragedy. Isn't something worse happening in Syria?

I yanked the hood up on my sweatshirt and just sat there, waiting for them to finish saying stuff to me.

TRULY

WHEN I CAME out of the bathroom, my older brother Henry said, "The awesome one in pigtails."

"What?" I asked. I mean, yeah, I had pigtails in, trying it out, not sure if maybe it looked babyish. It was the *awesome* part that seemed very un-Henry to say.

"In the *Odyssey*, Book 7, Athena disguises herself as a young girl. Homer describes her as 'the awesome one in pigtails.'"

"Oh," I said.

"As in 'the awesome one in pigtails led Odysseus through the city.' Remember that part?"

"Henry, I didn't read the whole—"

"Yes, you did."

"Well, that was last year, I don't—"

"Remember? And she was leading him through the—"

"Cool, Henry. I got it. Athena. That's not what I'm—"

"Your eyes *are* gray, like hers. Who are you helping escape?"

"Nobody," I told him. "But, Henry, do you think they look awesome? On me?"

"Your eyes?"

"The hair! The pigtails." I gave my head a little shake. "Or is it babyish? Come on, Henry. Tell me."

He shrugged and went back to whatever he was reading. I took the ponytail holders out. I didn't feel so awesome in them. Every time I try something more interesting with my hair than just wearing it flopped down around my face, it feels like I'm in some sort of costume. Like I'm a little kid again wearing Mom's nightgown, pretending to strut the red carpet in a gown at the Oscars.

"Who are you wearing?" Natasha would ask when we played red carpet.

"Ronzoni," I'd answer. "You?"

"Fig Newtons," she'd say, or something like that, both of us talking in whispery voices, pouting our lips toward wooden spoon–microphones while we watched ourselves in the mirror on the back of the bathroom door.

It's different in eighth grade, obviously. It's great, of course, especially now that I'm hanging around more with the Populars. Great but a little confusing. Natasha is so sweet, but then sometimes in a flash she's a little, well, kind of mean to me. But maybe I am being oversensitive. Hazel thinks I'm oversensitive and spoiled, even though she won't talk to me now and explain what she meant by that. Spoiled? What does that have to do with anything? How am I *spoiled*?

Mom said she thinks Hazel is just mad and jealous that I'm hanging around sometimes now with Natasha, and that's reasonable. The thought crossed my mind of saying *thank you, Captain Obvious* but of course I would never actually say that to anybody, especially Mom. I do think it's a pretty hilarious put-down, even though I felt kind of terrible when Natasha used it on me. But then she said it to Evangeline one time later this afternoon and Evangeline cracked up so I decided it's just a thing they all say to one another and I should not let it bother me.

It's hard when friends go in different directions, Mom was saying.

"I get that," I said instead of *thank you, Captain Obvious.* "And it's probably that much harder because Hazel hates Natasha."

"Does she?" Mom asked

"Totally," I said. "She has told me on many occasions that she can't believe I used to be best friends with Natasha when Natasha is such a shallow plate."

"A shallow . . ."

"Plate. I know. Whatever that means. One thing I am not missing so much now that Hazel isn't talking to me is her weird expressions."

Mom laughed at that. I like making her laugh.

That only thing that has me worrying that maybe Hazel is right, that I am spoiled and a not-nice person, is: Natasha used to say stuff like that to me about myself, too. One person could be just striking out, trying to say a hateful thing.

When it gets to be a chorus, maybe they're telling the truth?

Well, but. The fact is, Natasha used to say that critical stuff to me anytime I didn't want to play exactly what she wanted me to play. I had my suspicions I was not the one who was acting spoiled. According to Mom, Natasha was definitely the one who was spoiled when she made me cry so often in early elementary. But then again, Mom only heard my side of the story. And she was not used to dealing with friendship traumas because Henry is more of a keep-to-himself kind of kid.

I read some books about highly sensitive kids, and it's true I can't stand tags in my clothes or sudden noises and trage-dies, so maybe Natasha wasn't completely wrong. Or Hazel either.

It's funny they hate each other when they have some im-portant points of agreement over my faults. Or they used to. Natasha and I have made up now. Which feels really good. For almost two years I'd watch her in the halls and know she was going to pretend not to see me. I spent so much time, and so many fallen eyelashes and birthday candles, wishing it would not feel so awful between us anymore.

I went over to her house yesterday and it was such fun. We danced around in her room and took silly pictures of ourselves. The two of us dressed up in some of her dresses. She made me try on the pink and white one she wore to her aunt's wedding last spring. She stuffed socks in to make me look all filled out like her. It was hilarious. She asked me if I like Jack. Jack? I told her I've never had one conversation with him. She said she caught him smiling at me a few times today. "No way!" I shrieked, and we laughed about how silly Jack and I would look as a couple, him so tall and strong and me looking like a baby. We put on lipstick, full eyeliner, and tons of mascara and pretended to be seventeen, heading out to clubs, sticking out our tongues at the camera, pressing our faces cheek to cheek, pouting our lips. It was like a replay of being little kids playing dress-up, but the teen version.

"If you posted any of those," I told her, "my mom would kill me."

Natasha laughed and kissed my cheek. "No worries. Show me your sexiest pose!"

I tried.

"You are too pretty!" she yelled. "Why are you so photogenic? It's disgusting! I hate you!" But she was totally smiling and kidding. It felt really good, like my life was finally back on its track.

So today, I kept reminding myself of all those nice things Natasha said yesterday and told myself *Stop being oversensitive!* I have to toughen up if I want to chill with Natasha and those guys. Suck it up, Evangeline says, if anybody whines about a grade or catches a ball funny and jams her finger on the playground: suck it up and deal.

So I was telling myself *Suck it up!* after Natasha asked me "Talk much?" as we were leaving social studies this morning.

I had raised my hand in class a bunch and got called on three times. Maybe that's too much talking for an eighth grader, even if the topic was the Civil War and I love the Civil War. Henry and I watched the whole Ken Burns documentary on it more than once over the summer. But, okay, shut the heck up, I was realizing, too late. Was I acting like Hermione in the first Harry Potter book, before she got cool and popular? Because that would be bad. You don't want to be Book One Hermione. Books Five to Seven, yes. Not Book One.

I swallowed hard and didn't say anything back to Natasha. Instead I sucked it up and dealt.

"Don't let her bother you," Brooke whispered to me right then. "She's mad because Clay keeps staring at you."

"Oh, my goodness," I whispered back, both because, wow, really? Clay Everett was staring at me? Why? But also, yikes, she startled me, appearing suddenly beside me and whispering at me while being Brooke. I still wasn't fully used to being somebody Brooke would whisper to.

"Not that that excuses what a hair ball she's being, but . . ."

"No, it's fine," I said.

"Natasha is just—you know."

I didn't know. I mean I did, of course, but I wasn't sure I should be gossiping about her with Brooke. "Should I apologize, you think? Or . . ."

"For what?"

"For, you know. Clay?"

"Oh, yeah, definitely," Brooke said. "*Sorry your ex keeps staring at me.* That would be good."

It's not always easy for me to tell whether Brooke is just joking around. I'm still not completely fluent in the rhythm. But I tried teasing back. "How about if instead I said, *Sorry you're being such a hair ball*?"

Brooke laughed. "Perfect," she said.

HAZEL

TRULY SAT WITH *those people* again at lunch yesterday. It's becoming a bad habit. Something had to be done, and I was the girl to do it.

So first thing this morning, I waited at the cluster of lockers right near the center pole in the eighth-grade hall. That's where all *those people* have their lockers, bunched together. They smiled quizzically at me. I smiled back. Undeterred. I sat down in front of Brooke's locker cross-legged and waited.

When she finally showed up, I said, "Hi, how's it going, Brooke?"

"Great," she said. "You?" But she was looking at boy-wonder Clay, not at me. Maybe she was hoping he'd remember my name and mouth it to her.

"Great, thanks Brooke," I said, and then I asked her if she wanted to come over sometime.

All *those people* stopped breathing. It was a thing of beauty.

"Oh, uh, thanks," Brooke said. "That sounds great—but I'm really busy."

Every day from now on forever? I didn't ask.

I stood up and smiled again. As if I didn't get it, that I could not ask Brooke to come over. In what possible world could a middle-school nobody with a hunched-over, but still I do believe grand manner, just haul off and ask the number one most popular girl in the entire school to come over sometime?

Not the one we all live in.

Here in this world I cannot really even say hello to her. But to ask, Hey Brooke, how's it going. Do you want to come over sometime? Hahahaha! I might as plausibly have walked sideways across the lockers and spoken in Elvish.

But I did it. I asked her to come over sometime. Yup. Forced her to look all awkward. Brooke Armstrong, fidgeting. I did that.

"That's okay, Brooke," I told her, like I was used to just calling her by name, aloud, any old time. Three times so far.

Their mouths were hanging open, *those people,* their eyes darting between Brooke and me. Seeing me. If they'd noticed me at all, before, I probably only registered in their minds as that mild-mannered mildly depressed zero with the green hair. But now I was on their radar as that superweird girl who asked Brooke to come over to her house.

Good to meet you all.

"No worries, Brooke," I added. Four. I smiled at her. "Maybe sometime next week?"

"Sure," Brooke said. "That would be great."

"Yes," I said, "it will be," and walked away with all of them still watching.

BROOKE

ALL I KNEW about the girl who showed up at my locker today was she had green hair and she's in my math class. I couldn't even remember her name. Opal or Thelma or something. But she asked me over, and since I couldn't think of a good no, I said okay, sure, sometime.

All my friends were like *what?*

To be fair, she is one of those girls who stomps around in her heavy-soled boots and tights with holes, moody and awkward, and probably writes poetry in her notebooks during class about how nobody understands her. Not my usual pal. But my mom says, *You don't have to be friends with everybody, you just can't be unkind to anybody.*

So, whatever. Probably it'll never happen anyway.

First, though, everybody was coming over to my house, and how was I going to explain why both my parents were home? I really did not need to be explaining my family's private business to the whole world. Or even just my closest friends.

And no way this crew would not ask a lot of questions.

TRULY

THIS AFTERNOON a bunch of us went over to Brooke's house. Just "the girls"—Brooke (of course), Natasha, Evangeline, Lulu, and me. We went right to the kitchen because we were baking cookies for the eighth-grade bake sale tomorrow. Her parents were both home and they were so friendly and nice, just like Brooke. Happy to see a whole crew of us, but then they didn't hang around nervously helping get stuff out for us the way my parents do. They hadn't even prepared anything for us. Just, anything we wanted to get or do was fine. Then her mom went to drive Brooke's gorgeous older sister to ballet, and their dad and little brother went off somewhere on bikes. Everyone in Brooke's whole family has big happy smiles and dimples in their cheeks. They're all perfect.

After her parents left, we talked about science projects. We all complimented Lulu, whose presentation was today. She jumped around a little, she was so happy we all thought her bubbles went over well. She's very enthusiastic.

They all went *gross!* when I said my report was on dust mite feces. In a nice way, though. I sucked it up and dealt. I think it went pretty well. Might just take more practice, to be smooth and not feel lurchy in the face of their attention and joking. But I think I am improving. Instead of deciding to come up with a completely new science project tonight because mine is obviously too horrible, I said, "I know, gross, right? But sort of interesting? Maybe? I don't know. We'll see how many people puke when I give it tomorrow."

"I might puke now!" Lulu said. "Seriously? There's bug crap in dust? Ew!"

"Yes," I said.

"Okay, I fully have to stop eating dust as a snack," Brooke said.

We all laughed.

"But seriously, Truly," Lulu said. "I'm sure you'll do really good." Lulu is almost as small as me but much sturdier, with her shiny black hair all yanked back tight in a ponytail. Every time she talks I have to smile because she sounds like she sucked helium from a balloon.

"Thanks, Lulu," I said.

"You will," Evangeline agreed. "You're really good at oral reports. You make anything interesting."

"You're stressing me out!" I said. *They noticed me? Before?*

They laughed some more. Phew. Though I wasn't actually kidding. When I first saw Evangeline in sixth grade, I thought she was a teacher. She just seems so grown-up and in charge. She never talked to me directly until I started sitting at the Popular Table except one time in gym, when she yelled, "Get out of the way." Every time she talks to me now I flinch. But she only ever says super kind things to me. Still, she seems so sure of herself. And so tall.

"You'll do great," Brooke said. "How can you miss with bug turds and dust?"

"You'll probably get an A," Natasha said. "You always do."

"Hair flip," Evangeline said, and then demonstrated. Like a starlet deflecting compliments, she swished her braids off her face. I imitated her.

Brooke laughed.

We all flipped our hair like humble superstars a couple of times, then moved on and I was like, hallelujah. We talked about each person's science topic, made fun of it a little but then complimented the person. Then we talked a bit about our History Day project. Everybody liked my idea of Benedict Arnold. "Maybe we could do like a skit about what he did," I suggested.

"That could be really cool," Lulu said.

"Definitely," Brooke agreed. "Write a short play, and we'd all have parts?"

"That's sick!" Evangeline said.

"Oh," I said, dying instantly on the spot. "I mean, no. Of course. I didn't—"

"No, I meant that sounds awesome," Evangeline said. "Sick like great!"

"Oh," I said. "Right. Of course." I did a hair flip.

Brooke laughed.

"A play could be really fun," Lulu said.

"True," Brooke said. "Practicing it and all that. Great. Lulu, hand me the cookie sheet?"

"Yeah!" Lulu said. "Here. So what exactly happened with Benedict Arnold? In history? Revolutionary War, right?"

"Yeah," I said. "The thing that I think is cool about the story is that Benedict was a great soldier, but he wasn't good at getting along with people. The only one who really liked him was George Washington. And then Benedict betrayed him."

"Way to win friends," Natasha said.

"Well, from what I've read, I mean . . ." I didn't want to sound like a know-it-all, like Natasha used to accuse me of being. "I don't know."

"No, what do you think?" Brooke asked, leaning forward.

I took a deep breath. "I think Benedict thought if he turned over West Point to the British, he could end the war. The war wasn't so popular right then—so many soldiers who were basically only teenagers dying, you know. He could bring peace, and be a hero."

"Huh," Lulu said, banging flour through the sifter into the big metal bowl beneath. "I thought he was just a traitor."

"That's what . . ." *Am I talking too much?* "I mean, most people think that, but . . ."

"We could show the other side?" Brooke asked.

I shrugged.

"I love it," Brooke said.

I felt my face heating up.

"Plus it's Colonial," said Evangeline. "So we can just wear sweats and hike the elastic part up to our knees, and do long socks. Right?"

"Yeah!" said Lulu.

"I have a dress," Natasha said. "From my aunt's wedding in the spring. I was a bridesmaid."

"It's really pretty," I said.

"So you automatically get to be the girl?" Evangeline asked Natasha. Then she turned to me. "Is there even a girl? History sucks, leaving women out so much."

"Peggy," I said. "Peggy Shippen. Benedict Arnold's wife. Natasha could be Peggy. Shippen." *Ugh. Too much!* I shrugged, like, *or maybe that's not her name! Just saying random names because why would I know that Benedict Arnold's wife's name is Peggy Shippen? That's weird! Hahaha! Oh help.*

"I don't think you'd fit into the dress," Natasha said to Evangeline. "You can try if you want but . . ."

"Youch," Lulu squeaked.

"I didn't mean anything . . ." Natasha said quickly.

"So wait—there's George Washington, Benedict, Peggy—that's only three," Brooke said.

I considered telling her the other parts that could be possibilities but decided to hold back. "There have to be others," I said. "I'll work on it."

"We should split up the research," Evangeline said.

"Definitely," Lulu agreed.

"Cool," Brooke said. "Evangeline, is that butter blended yet?"

"Yeah," Evangeline said. "Here."

"Dump in that flour stuff?" Brooke told Lulu. Then she turned back to me. "That sounds really good. The untold story. Friendship and betrayal. Awesome."

"Yeah," Natasha agreed, bumping me with her hip. "What could be better than friendship and betrayal, right?"

"Right," I said. "Sure."

NATASHA

"WHAT COULD BE better than friendship and betrayal," I joked. "Right?"

"Right," Truly answered nervously. "Sure."

"Yo, Brooke," Evangeline said, giving up momentarily fighting me on who should get to wear *my* dress in the History Day play Truly was fully going to write for us, thanks to me. "How small are those cookies?"

"How small are *your* cookies?" Brooke answered without looking up.

Lulu laughed. "How small is your *face*?"

"How face is your small?" I said. Lulu flashed me a smile. We love random disses. Poor Truly was looking a bit frantic. She wasn't used to us yet.

"Your face is small cookies," Evangeline said.

"Your cookies are small faces, *what!*" Brooke said. "I was thinking we should make a lot of smallies for the bake sale, no?"

"Yeah, good idea," Lulu said. "Maybe three in a bag for a buck?"

"Or four," I said. "So they'll sell out first. We don't want to be the losers whose stuff doesn't sell."

"That would be sad," Lulu said.

"Like when I was in first grade?" I said. "My dad burned the cookies and he made me bring them in anyway. Remember that, Truly?"

"Vaguely," Truly said. A lie. I know she remembered. She brought cupcakes. They were perfect.

"I'll never forget it," I said, rolling my eyes. "We had to stand there in front of our stuff and mine were these hard lumps of coal, and nobody bought them."

Everybody went *awww*. This is what's so good about being older, and having good friends. The humiliating stories aren't shameful anymore—they're funny, and good for bonding. Also, sympathy. *I'm such a loser* is code for cool.

I pouted out my bottom lip. I have nice lips, Mom once said. "Ms. Berger bought five dollars' worth at the end."

"She was so nice," Truly agreed. "Ms. Berrrrgerrrrr."

"I threw out the rest," I said. "Of course my mom was sure I ate them all. As if."

Brooke shook her head at that. "Ugh," she said. She knows my mom is not the easiest person to deal with, and she's pretty supportive about it. I mean, I know it's way worse that Lulu's mom died, but we're not in some sort of pity competition. It's hard to have a difficult mom, too. But Evangeline flashed me that look like *shut up about mothers in front of Lulu.*

As if suddenly I am such an insensitive clod I would forget that.

"These cookies?" Evangeline said, tasting some batter. "No way people will pass these babies up. Three in a bag's probably fine. Yum."

"My dad's recipe," said Brooke.

"The man's a genius," Lulu squeaked. Everybody smiled at her.

Truly tasted a tiny bit, finally. "Yum," she said. Her mom doesn't allow her to taste raw batter.

"But how about a couple of biggies for us, for now," Lulu squealed.

"Nice!" Brooke said.

"Yes," yelled Evangeline. "Biggies! I call I get to be Benedict Arnold."

"I think Truly should decide who gets which part," I said generously. "I mean, doing the play was her idea."

"Oh, anything's fine with me," Truly said.

"You are such a sweet person!" Lulu said.

"Me?" Truly and I both asked.

Everybody laughed at that.

"I meant Truly," Lulu said, and giggled her high-pitched honking giggle.

I pouted again. They laughed a bit, but still it was like they were ganging up on me. I was the one trying to be nice, and they were just purposely ignoring me and making it like

Truly was so great, and Lulu was so tragic, and Evangeline so boss, and of course Brooke is still and always on top. What about *me?*

"I *told* you Truly was awesome, didn't I?" I was smiling but inside I was, like, *Why does nothing go my way for more than five-second stretches?*

"She is," Evangeline agreed. "Truly is the sweetest kid in the whole grade." She took another lump of dough to eat. "So. I get to be Benedict. Right, Truly?"

Truly laughed. "Okay."

"Hey, Evangeline . . ." I said.

"Yeah?" Evangeline asked, with the big hunk of dough in her mouth, which made Brooke laugh.

"Maybe you should save a little dough for the cookies?"

Everybody all got quiet at that. Okay it came out way harsher than I meant it to. I was just trying to get back to joking around. She didn't have to look at me like I was threatening her puppy with a switchblade. Come on.

"Youch," Brooke said, after a minute. "Chill, huh, Natasha?"

"What? I'm kidding," I said, smiling at them all. "Right, Truly?"

Truly shrugged, imitating Brooke.

"Stop trying to be a mini-Brooke," I told her.

She opened her pale eyes all innocent at me. "What?" Truly asked.

I opened my eyes super wide like her, and imitated her Brooke-like shrug.

Truly looked at the floor. Busted.

Lulu said, "Natasha, man, did you sit on a fan this morning or what? Why are you being such a pill?"

I smiled at Lulu. "I'm just joking around. Can't anybody here take a joke?"

"Tell one and we'll laugh," Evangeline said. "Otherwise shut your trap." She got up and went to the bathroom.

"Jeez, Louise, some people take everything personally," I said.

"Preach," Lulu said.

"Right?" I asked her.

"I was talking about you," Lulu said, all stony faced.

"Truly knows I was joking around," I said, trying not to panic.

"Of course," Truly said. "I'm sure you were."

"See?" I asked. But I am not at all sure they did see.

JACK

WALKING DOWN TO lunch, she was next to me. She comes up to my armpit. I have known her since sixth grade and always noticed her, but never talked to her, never before today, anyway. She has a really sweet smile.

As we were walking along I was thinking, this is the time to say something to her. Right now. I had a good thing to say, too. I was thinking I could say: "Hey, Truly—I really liked your dust mite feces report today."

Some people kept going "ew" while Truly was giving her presentation, but I thought it was really interesting. I will never look at dust the same way again. Dust won't be just little puffs of fluff to me now. It will be little puffs of fluff with a lot of tiny bug poop in it. That's how good her presentation was this morning.

I wanted to tell her that.

I couldn't. No words came out.

Truly is tiny, but she was walking very quickly, chatting

with her friends Brooke and Natasha as they skittered toward the cafeteria.

I sat down at my usual table, at the end with the other sporty boys. They all got quiet as I unzipped my lunch box. I am famous for my lunches. I make them myself, because it's like an interest of mine, a hobby, and besides my mom used to rush it. Just slap some meat on bread, throw a can of soda crushingly on top. It's not her fault. She has enough to do, and she is one of those people who doesn't care that much about food.

I make Mom's lunch now sometimes, too, whenever she wants. Otherwise she just has a yogurt and a banana, for her whole meal. The people in her office where she works are always impressed on days when she takes a lunch I made her. At least that's what my mom says. But she's like that, complimentary. Especially of me.

Truly Gonzales didn't used to sit at our table, but since she started to, I've noticed that she takes the same thing for lunch every day: two slices of turkey on white bread, no crusts, probably mayonnaise, plus one vanilla wafer cookie. For me, her whole lunch would be a small beige appetizer.

I pulled my sandwich from the bag. Some of the guys were getting impatient. I unwrapped the foil and said, "Pumpernickel."

Mike Shimizu nodded. He makes his own lunch, too, and takes it as seriously as I do. He's my best friend with the possible exception of Clay Everett, but unlike me and Dave and even Clay, who's medium height and a bit skinny, Mike is sort of a runty guy, real small, so he just can't eat all that much. He does like interesting food, though, you gotta give Mike that. Not Clay, man—he doesn't care, he'll just eat anything. He doesn't even have a favorite food. One time he was over and my mom asked him what he likes, so she could get it for him. She's like that, always wanting to get people stuff they like. Clay said he liked everything. She asked him if he was home and could eat anything he wanted, what would he chose? Clay said usually he just opens the refrigerator and starts eating from the front and goes on eating until he's full.

My mom thought that was awesome. I do, too. Clay's like that, completely likeable. The only thing is, he doesn't have as much appreciation for the genius of my mad food skills as a result.

I held up the sandwich so everybody at the lunch table could see.

"Tell us," Dave said. He appreciates excellence.

I told them: mesquite wood-smoked turkey, aged sharp Adirondack cheddar (one slice), deseeded cucumbers, sliced grape tomatoes, one roasted red pepper marinated in olive oil and capers overnight, cracked black pepper, and Dijon mustard.

Some kids said, "Mmm." A couple guys down by the end shook their heads at each other. They don't get it. Beside me on the bench, Mike was nodding. "Unbelievable," he said. "The pepper."

"Yeah," I said. "I've been working on the balance. Last week I overdid it on the capers."

"No," said Mike. "The cracked black pepper. That's exactly right. It needs that, for the bite. I wouldn't have thought of the cracked black pepper."

Mike looked sadly down at his own spread. He'd done an old favorite: poached salmon on seven grain with tomato. Absolutely delicious, no question, but he had brought it last Monday, too.

We both nodded.

I popped open my club soda and took a swig, then started to eat. I was really hungry. The balance on the marinade was way better than last week's.

I finished before Mike but waited for him before we went out to the lower playground. It's basically a parking lot without cars and a few basketball hoops without nets, but it's perfect for us. We're in eighth grade; we don't need swings and slides, all that, anymore—just a good open stretch of concrete with a fence around it, below window level so the teachers inside can't spy on us. The teachers on lunch duty mostly stay up top, with the sixth and seventh graders.

By the time we got out there, Dave Calderon and Lulu Peters were already captains, choosing up sides for Salugi, this game we invented back in sixth grade. Basically you have to get to your goal without being thrown down, and then, the modification we added this year, now that we have control of the lower playground. You have to get *through* the goal. It gives the smaller kids a role, like kickers or wide receivers in football. The goals are these little spaces under the fence out there. The small kids are good for that, because the bigger kids like me, Clay, Dave Calderon, and Evangeline Murphy would never fit through those tiny holes. Though we are good at grabbing the smaller kids' feet and yanking them so they can't get through. Salugi has been officially banned ever since Evangeline gave Mike a bloody nose last year, but we play anyway. It's a really fun game, and a little collision with concrete never hurt anyone.

Much.

Well, not until today.

Lulu picked me, so Dave got Mike. Mike is a great guy and really smart at school, up there in the top group with Truly in every subject, and a really nice person, too. But he will never go pro in Salugi.

I am not in the top class of math this year. I guess I didn't do so well at it last year, or on the state tests last May. My mom says that's okay, but of course she's like that.

We lined up in the center of the playground and started. It was a hot day, still summery even though it was almost October, so I was sweating pretty soon. I love Salugi. The game was going really well, lots of interceptions, well-balanced teams. Evangeline is very strong, probably the best athlete in the grade. She forced a couple of fumbles in the first few minutes, but Lulu made a great catch and faked out Evangeline beautifully, then tossed the ball to me. Clay almost intercepted, but I caught it and started toward the goal. Lulu sprinted ahead, shouting, "Jack! Jack!" ready to get the last-second pass from me.

I knew we were going to score. I could already see exactly

how I'd block Dave away from Lulu's feet after she caught the pass from me.

I had maybe three of their defenders hanging on me. I'm strong, though, and I'd just eaten that really great sandwich—I could still taste the clean of the cucumbers blending with the smokiness of the turkey—so I was well energized. I focused on Lulu's feet—just get to those white Keds with the blue laces and we'll be up one-zip. That's what I was saying to myself when I decided to kick it up a notch and, dipping my right shoulder to lose one of their pesky defenders, plowed smack into Truly Gonzales.

What she was doing in midfield I have no idea. She never used to play Salugi. I don't know when she started. All week I was noticing her out there. What she does during the game is, she stands around until the action comes near her and then does this skittering thing with her tiny steps to get away.

Only this time she didn't get away.

I hit her with the full force of my shoulder on her back.

I'm not saying it was her fault. Not at all. I should've seen her there, near the sideline. I read somewhere that great ball-players can see the entire field at all times. But I didn't see her until I'd already slammed into her.

She went way up in the air before she slammed into the concrete a few feet downfield.

Everybody crowded around. I still had the ball tucked into the crook of my arm, no fumble.

"You okay?" Brooke asked her.

Truly blinked her pale eyes twice, then smiled slightly at Brooke.

"Oh, no!" Mike screamed. "Look at her knee! Ew!"

All of us, including Truly, looked at her knees. One of them was fine. The other was not. It was cracked open. It wasn't bleeding that much, but there was gook in it and under the gook, something hard-looking and white, maybe the bone.

I think that's when some kids started screaming.

Truly's face went from surprised and pink to blueish white. She made a little sound in the back of her throat.

I dropped the ball and without really thinking it through, picked her up. I didn't want her to faint right there on the lower playground. "Time-out," I mumbled as I carried Truly toward school.

She rested her very pale face against my shoulder and closed her eyes. I know this is selfish of me, when I should've been focused more on sympathy about her bashed-open leg, but her head on my sweaty T-shirt felt nice.

"Sorry," I whispered. First thing I ever said to her: sorry.

She didn't answer. You can't blame her. It's gotta be hard to work up any politeness toward the guy who just completely crushed you in Salugi, even if it was an accident and he's sorry.

I didn't say anything else, just carried her to the nurse's office. The nurse wasn't there. Some sixth-grader lying on a cot with an ice pack on his nose said the nurse had gone to the teachers' room and would be right back. I wasn't sure what to do with Truly, where to put her—the kid with the nose had closed his eyes, so he was definitely in no hurry to give up his spot on the cot. I wasn't sure if Truly would want to be put on one of the plastic chairs or not. She still had her head on my sweaty T-shirt, so I just stood there holding her.

She is very tiny but my arms were starting to lose their grip. I didn't want to drop her on the floor so I had to shift around a little bit. Truly's eyes opened and she stared right into my face. She seemed surprised to find me there.

"I like . . ." I started. "I liked your . . . bugs. That poop in dust. Thing."

"What?"

"Project. Report," I said. "Today. Science. Poop. Bug poop."

A drop of sweat fell off my forehead onto her nose. I tried to wipe it away quickly so she wouldn't notice it but I almost dropped her, moving my arm like that and maybe almost slapping her on the nose.

"Sorry," I said again. I quickly hiked her up but she sort of yelped at being tossed around like that. I stopped moving. She wiped the sweat ball off her nose herself and asked, "Dust mite feces?"

I nodded slightly. I didn't want to shake any more sweat balls loose.

"It didn't gross you out?" Truly asked.

"No," I whispered.

She stared at me for a few seconds, then smiled a bit and said, "Thanks."

I forgot I should say you're welcome until she closed her eyes and lowered her head onto my shoulder again. By then it was too late.

The nurse came back after another minute or two. She took one look at Truly's knee and said, "Uh-oh." I could feel Truly starting to breathe faster at that.

The nurse said, "You can put her down and go back to class now, Jack."

I said, "That's okay."

The nurse called Truly's mom, sent Nose Boy back to his class, and told me to lay Truly down on the cot. I shook my head.

"I ate a big lunch," I said, trying to explain why I wouldn't run out of strength. The nurse looked very confused at that, but I saw a small smile on Truly's mouth. She has such a sweet smile. She wasn't too heavy at all. I could've stood there in the nurse's office holding Truly Gonzales until the end of time.

TRULY GONZALES ⌄

2 hrs • 🗨️

I got 10 stitches plus an internal running stitch. And a double scoop of ice cream on the way home. #YOLO

Like • Get Notifications • Promote • Share • Edit

👍 **37 people** like this comment.

Brooke Armstrong, Natasha Lawrence, Lulu Peters, and **34** others like this.

Hazel Leary Are you okay? Call me.
September 28 at 6:17pm 👍 Like

Jack Williams Sorry 🙁
September 28 at 6:18pm 👍 Like • 7

Clay Everett that's horrible/nice!
September 28 at 6:19 👍 Like • 9

Natasha Lawrence Oh noooooooo! 😲
September 28 at 6:19 👍 Like • 1

CLAY

Hey Brooke.

You still up? I can't sleep.

I had to talk Jack down off the roof after he saw what Truly posted. He and I were going to brainstorm History Day ideas but I told him I got this. So I really have to come up with something. Ykwim? The poor guy was ready to go over to her house and set himself on fire on her lawn or something.
As penance.

I was thinking, tho, while we were talking—you could pretty much get through life saying only these 3 things:
1. That's horrible!
2. Nice!
3. Hmmm.
Not that you'd want to, but like if you had to pack light.

After I got off the phone with Jack I called Natasha, because she had called and texted and Snapchatted me and all that stuff a bunch of times while I was talking to Jack. I was planning to just blow her off and get going on History Day ideas + algebra homework, but then I was like, yeah right.
I'm so not gonna do that.

Also I was thinking I could prbly completely calm her down if I limited myself to the 3 things. How much trouble cd I get in saying only that's horrible, nice, and hmmm?

How do I not know yet that the answer to HOW MUCH TROUBLE COULD I MAKE FOR MYSELF is always SO MUCH FRIGGING MORE THAN I REALIZE?

"So you obviously know why I'm mad at you, right?" Natasha asked me.

I said, HMMMM.

Then she yelled at me for a while until I had to abandon the 3 things plan because it was just pissing her off way more. How much do I hate TALKING on the phone? I asked if we could move to texting or whatever. Yeah. That worked. Not.

Natasha yelled at me that I should stop pretending to be all innocent. She wouldn't say of what.

My question to you: Did I kill somebody while I wasn't paying attention?

I really have to focus. ☹ between random murders and cracking my knuckles I'm doomed.

Then she hung up on me. So. Guess my work here is done. Everybody's pissed at me. I may as well go to bed.

Can you meet me by the lockers early? And bring your discard list of History Day ideas? I know you gotta have something. Jack might bring scones. The guy is srsly messed UP. Though messed up w/scones is so much better than messed up w/o scones. Right?

I really wish you were still awake.

BROOKE

TODAY WAS THE DAY. That girl I told okay sure let's hang sometime, Hazel, lives near school, so we walked. We didn't have a lot to talk about on the way, but she didn't seem to mind. She was telling me that when she grows up she wants to be a humanitarian and a movie star, and travel all over the world very glamorously and live life to the hilt. She asked if I like to live life to the hilt.

"I mostly just hang around," I said.

"But when you get older, and you can do anything," she whispered as we began climbing the steep steps up to her huge stone house. "What do you like to imagine?"

I shrugged.

"Like, I am constantly imagining I can fly," said Hazel, spreading her arms wide. "Do you ever imagine you're flying?"

"Um," I said. "I sometimes imagine I forgot to wear pants to school."

"Today is my half-birthday," she said, pulling a key out of her shirt. It had been hanging from a shoelace around her neck, along with another key, a tiny one. She bent close to the lock to use the bigger key. "Are you thirteen and a half yet?"

I shook my head.

"It feels, you just feel . . . older, at thirteen and a half," she said. "Things shift, subtly. You'll see."

I followed her in. Her house might actually be a mansion. The ceiling was very, very far from the floor in the room where you walk in. In my house and all my friends' houses, there's a front hall or just a where-you-walk-in. Hazel's house had like a lobby. On the left there was a huge square room that was maybe a library. Anyway there were tons of books in there, on dark shelves all the way up to the ceiling. At the far end of the library two huge doors opened into some other room. I didn't know what room it was or if that one would open to another huge room. I decided to stay close to Hazel to avoid getting lost.

Hazel unzipped her jacket and dropped it on the floor, with her backpack still hooked through the sleeves. I hadn't worn a jacket because it was pretty warm out still, and I sweat a lot. I put my backpack down next to Hazel's, then followed Hazel past a dining room that had paintings of annoyed-looking people hanging on the greenish walls, through a long hallway, into the massive kitchen.

"What do you want for a snack?"

I didn't know.

Hazel climbed up onto one of the metal counters and opened a cabinet. "Let's have Mallomars," she said. "I think you can tell a lot about a person by the way she eats Mallomars, don't you?"

She brought down the box and held it open for me to choose one. I picked one in the center of the back row, wondering what that revealed about me. She took one from the far right front and said, "Come meet my bird, Sweet Pea. Did I tell you I've had him since I turned three?"

My Mallomar was melting a little on my fingers as I hurried to keep up with Hazel, around corners and then up, up, up a steep flight of stairs with dark red carpeting worn out in the center of each step. My house is just regular. I'd never been anyplace like Hazel's house.

"Sweet Pea is a budgerigar," Hazel was explaining. "People think that's the same as a parakeet, but it's not. Budgies are slightly larger and much more exotic. Do you like exotic animals?"

"Um," I said.

"I got Sweet Pea when I was three years old and though tragically he never learned to talk people-language, he is still able to communicate, at least to me. I can tell his chirps apart. You'll see. This is my brother's room—don't go there," she warned, indicating a closed door.

"Okay," I said.

"This is the bathroom—do you have to go?"

"No."

"That's fine. Tell me when you do."

I took a bite of my Mallomar, revealing that I was a hungry type of person.

Hazel gripped a doorknob on a tall white door. "And this—this is my room."

She swung the door open. Everything inside was pink. Pink carpeting, pink walls, pink bed piled high with pink pillows. "Sweet Pea?" she called, heading across the thick rug toward an empty birdcage. "Sweet Pea? Ahhh!!!!"

I got there as she began screaming, and saw a dead bird, lying on its side in the bottom of the cage.

She was still screaming when a woman raced into the room, across the acres of pink rug, and grabbed Hazel, demanding, "What happened, love?"

Hazel stopped screaming, said, "Sweet Pea . . . died!" and started to sob.

The woman was an older version of Hazel—big brown eyes, freckled nose. Hazel's hair is dyed green on the tips, but the woman had just black hair all the way down, pulled back in a bun. She gathered Hazel into her arms and sat down on the rug, hugging her.

"Oh, Mommy," Hazel wailed. "He's dead!"

"Shh," the mom hushed.

I was still standing there, holding my melting Mallomar. I don't think the mom even noticed I was in the room.

Hazel's crying turned from shrieks to gasps to, finally, just little burbles that sounded like she was saying "Haboo."

Her mom was stroking her hair whispering "OK," and occasionally checking her watch.

I ate the rest of my Mallomar and tried not to look at the dead bird or Hazel and her mom, who seemed to be having some private time, just with me happening to be standing three feet away. I would've gone to the bathroom to hide or at least wash off my chocolate-coated fingers, but Hazel had said to tell her before I went there, so I thought maybe their family had a rule of some sort about that. They seemed like they might.

Hazel sniffled hard, and then said, "I've had him since I was three." She whimpered a little before she dried her face on the bottom of her T-shirt. "It feels, it just feels like, like the death of my childhood."

Hazel started sobbing again.

"Oh, sweetheart," said the mom.

"Maybe I should call my dad," I whispered.

"Don't leave!" screamed Hazel.

So I didn't.

"I feel like . . ." she started again. "I feel like maybe Sweet Pea felt like, like I had grown up, now that I turned thirteen and a half—and so he felt like, after all this time, this lifetime together . . . he . . ." She was too breathy to continue.

"Hazel," said the mother. "There's something I have to tell you."

Hazel sat up straight, slid off her mother's lap, and sat cross-legged on the carpeting facing her mom. She swallowed hard and then nodded.

"Sweet Pea," started the mom. "Sweet Pea wasn't actually, well, what you think he is. Or was."

"What do you mean?" asked Hazel.

"You didn't get this bird on your third birthday."

"Yes, I did," Hazel protested. "I remember. I went to the pet store with Grammy and Papa, and picked him out."

"Well," said the mom, tilting her head sideways. "You picked out a bird. He looked something like Sweet Pea, and his name was Sweet Pea, too . . ."

"You mean . . ."

The mom scrunched her face apologetically. "You were so excited, but then the stupid bird died a few weeks after we got him, and, well, we didn't want to start explaining death to a high-strung three-year-old—so I just went back to the pet store and got a new one."

"I can't believe you."

"Well," said the mom. "We didn't want you to be sad. And when that second one died you were five, and a week into kindergarten which was *not* going smoothly for you, remember, so that seemed like a bad time to deal with death, too. You were a baby! So I just bought a new parakeet."

"Budgie."

"Isn't that the same as a parakeet?"

Hazel stared at her mother. "Budgies are more . . . Sweet Pea was a budgie."

"Not recently."

"There was more than one replacement?"

The mom smiled awkwardly. "Sweet Pea was sort of a series of birds."

"*No!*"

"Honey," said the mom, leaning toward Hazel. "Some of them were green, some were blue . . ."

"You said he was molting!" shrieked Hazel. "Get out! Get out of my room! I want to be alone with Sweet Pea, or whoever this is! Get out!"

I wasn't sure if I was supposed to stay or go. I followed the mom out. Hazel didn't yell at me to stay, so I figured I'd made the right choice.

The mom closed the door behind us and said, "Do you want a snack? I'm studying for the bar."

I had no idea what that meant. I shook my head.

"You can wait in the kitchen," she said, moving fast toward the stairs. I could see where Hazel gets her speed. "I'm sure Hazel will be down soon."

When we got down to the kitchen, the mom took out two glasses and a pitcher of water. She poured us each some, gulped hers down, and then looked at me. "It's nice for Hazel that you're here. She was bound to discover death eventually, and it's nice she has a friend to lean on."

"I'm not really . . . we're not that close," I explained. "I just sit next to her in math."

"Well," said the mom, pouring herself more water. "I wish I could chat, but as I said I really have to study. Call me if you and Hazel need anything."

She left. I sat alone in the humongous kitchen, listening to the clock tick, wondering if I should call my dad and ask him to pick me up early. Last year my brother picked me up from friends' houses on his way home from team practices. Just as

I was walking out of the kitchen to get my phone, though, Hazel appeared in the doorway. She had a small jewelry box in her hands.

"Is that the kind where, when you open it, tinkly music plays and a ballerina spins on her toe?" I asked.

"Yes," Hazel said.

"I had one of those when I was little," I said.

"Want to do a funeral?" Hazel asked.

"Is he in there?" I asked.

Hazel nodded.

I followed her through the kitchen out into the huge backyard. Across a big green lawn, up a hill toward some evergreen trees, we came to a shed. "Hold this," said Hazel, and she handed me the jewelry box/coffin.

"Oh," I said, "Um, okay."

I waited outside the shed while she went in. I tried to be very still so I wouldn't drop it, thinking about the dead bird body just inches from my fingers. Hazel came out wearing big green gloves and holding a small shovel.

"Ready to do this?" she asked me.

"I don't have any experience with death," I admitted.

"I didn't think I did, either," said Hazel. "I guess you never know."

"Good point."

I followed her to the evergreen trees. She knelt down beside one and started digging. I just stood there, carefully holding the jewelry box/coffin. When she was done, she said, "You can put him in."

"Maybe you should," I suggested. "You're the one, you know . . ."

"That's okay," she said.

So I placed the box into the hole.

"Kneel down with me," she whispered. "Please? I'll be quick."

I knelt in the soft dirt. Usually at a friend's house we play Ping-Pong or bake or watch stuff online.

"I'm going to say some stuff, okay?"

I nodded.

Hazel took a deep breath. "Good-bye, Sweet Pea. I'm sorry I didn't realize you were actually a series of birds. I'm sorry I wasn't a good enough bird-owner, and you never learned to talk and you never flew anyplace interesting. You obviously had a boring and misunderstood life. I'm so sorry." She sniffled.

I was thinking she might start really crying again, and if she did, where would I find her mother? But she cleared her throat and turned to me. "Do you want to say anything?"

"Uh-uh."

"You can. Just say whatever comes to mind."

"I'm not that good at saying things," I whispered.

"That's okay," whispered Hazel. "He can't really hear you anyway."

I turned and looked at her. She was sort of smiling at me. I sort of smiled back. Hazel closed her eyes and lowered her head again.

I took a deep breath and said, "Um. Sweet Pea? Hi. Or . . .

I mean, I guess . . . good-bye. Sorry. Too soon?"

"No," Hazel said. "That's right. Good-bye. Good night, Sweet Pea. And flights of angels something something. Keep going, Brooke. Please."

"Okay." I closed my eyes and wished for words to come and giggles to not. "So, uh, Sweet Pea. I never knew you, you know, alive, and I honestly don't know Hazel that well either—but, um, I think she really, kind of, loved you."

"I did," mumbled Hazel with her eyes closed. "I did."

"So, yeah," I continued without a clue. "Well. Um. So. I was thinking maybe it would be nice, if you could, like, maybe show up in her dream some night, and fly with her. Because Hazel likes to imagine she's flying. Anyway, um, thank you for, well, that's all."

Hazel stayed still with her eyes closed, so I didn't get up either. I wondered how long we were going to be kneeling there, and if we were supposed to be praying. Sometime after my feet fell asleep, Hazel stood up and shoveled the dirt onto the top of the box and patted it down hard. I stood up while she was doing that. She drooped beside the grave with her eyes closed and her gloved wrists crossed on the shovel's handle for a while. I kept my head down and waited, resisting the urge to stamp my pin-cushiony feet. Eventually, she went back to the shed. I waited outside it again until she came out without the gloves and shovel.

"Thanks," she said as we headed back toward her house. "That was really beautiful, what you said."

"Oh," I said. "Okay. Good."

She held the back door open for me. "Is this the worst afternoon of your life?"

"It's . . . different."

She laughed a short blurty laugh and then snorted it in.

We waited out front for my dad to pick me up. I sat between my stuff and Hazel. We both kicked the backs of our feet against the stone wall. When my dad's car pulled up, I turned to Hazel. "Happy half-birthday," I said.

"Thank you," she answered. "Kind of hard to have a happy half-birthday when tragedy intrudes, but thank you for the thought."

"You're welcome."

I grabbed my stuff and ran down the steps to my dad. I slipped into the front seat of the car, buckled my seat belt, and leaned over to get my kiss.

"Did you have a good time?" Dad asked.

I shrugged. As we pulled away, I looked out the window. Up the hill, on the front lawn, Hazel was running around in big, loose circles, her arms spread straight out.

90

NATASHA

TO CELEBRATE GETTING the okay on our History Day projects, and just because it was a random Tuesday, a bunch of us decided to walk into town after school.

"Walk?" Truly asked, her gray eyes going wide. "Into town?"

"You don't have to if you don't want to," I told her. I smiled, though, to stop myself from saying, *Could you just cool it about your stupid freaking knee already you spoiled baby you are not the first person on the planet ever to get stitches.*

"No, I want to," she said. "I just, I have to call home and ask."

"Her parents are very overprotective," I explained to everybody.

"Cool," Brooke said. "Whatever. We could just ditch the town thing if that's a problem."

Everybody smiled at Brooke. Like she was the only considerate person. Like she really was George Washington, not just playing him in our stupid History Day play that Truly was somehow the boss of, when she was supposed to be like the little worker bee. Hooray for Brooke, the nicest person in the country. When I'm the one who had just said two nice things to/about Truly.

"Hi, Brooke," called the weird green-haired girl I rescued Truly from.

"Hey, Hazel," Brooke said. "All good?"

"I'm managing," Hazel answered, schlumping past us.

"Her pet bird died," Brooke explained.

"Aw," Lulu said. "Poor thing."

"That sucks," Evangeline said. "Any pet dying. And a bird . . . huh. Does it just, like, fall off the perch or what?"

"It was stiff in the bottom of the cage," Brooke said.

"Ew," Clay said. "You saw it?"

"I helped bury it," Brooke said.

"Seriously?" Lulu asked.

Brooke nodded. "She's . . . unusual, Hazel. But . . . interesting. Kind of deep. And funny."

"Maybe she's just a wacko," I suggested.

"Nice," Clay said. "Way to care. Her pet just died." Then he looked over to where Truly was standing, hunched over her phone, her face near the bricks of the school.

"Meanwhile," I said, in my most sympathetic voice, all full of *awww* like Lulu was for the weird girl, "poor Truly. Her parents. Seriously, I'm surprised they don't send her to school wrapped in bubble paper."

"We'd pop her all day," Theo said.

"Step back," Jack said. "Don't be a creeper."

"What?" Theo said. "I wasn't trying to—bubble paper. Who can resist popping bubble wrap?"

"Not me," Mike Shimizu said. "I'd stomp that stuff anytime."

"Pigs," Lulu said in her squeaky voice.

"What?" Theo protested. "I don't get it."

"You guys have dirty minds," Mike said. "We're actually talking about bubble wrap."

"Speaking of—I need some serious bubble tea," Evangeline said. "Have you guys tried that place yet?"

"Gross," Clay said. "I tried that this summer! It's horrible. It's like gobs of goo and they shoot up the straw into your mouth like snot bullets."

"Snot bullets," Lulu shrieked. She started laughing her squeaky, snorty laugh. "Now I definitely want some."

"Who looked at tea," Clay asked Lulu, "and thought, you know what this stuff needs? Snot bullets."

She doubled over squeak-laughing at that.

"Seriously," I agreed, trying to be positive. Lulu is not the only positive person on the planet. "And then the snot bullets smack your . . . you know, when you suck them up the straw and, wham, they hit your . . . you know."

Everybody looked blankly at me.

"The little dongy thing in the back of your throat," I said.

"You have a dongy thing in the back of your throat?" Evangeline asked.

"Thanks for sharing," Lulu said. She was acting all rude to me, I knew, because she got stuck being the French guy in the History Day play. Lulu's dad is a marine, so she fully did not want to be the French traitor, but tough. Could be worse; Truly took the lousy housemaid part for herself. I'm not the one in charge of giving out parts, obviously, though, so if Lulu wanted to be pissy she should take it out on Truly.

"Dongy thing," Theo said. "Heh heh heh. Dongy thing."

Oh, please.

Truly limped back to us and hovered at the edge of the circle, quivering like a hummingbird. I turned to her and smiled. "Everything okay, Truly?"

"I can come!" Truly said. What a triumph. Hurray. "My mom said she'll pick me up at five thirty at the pizza place, is that okay?"

"Sure," I said. "Hey, Truly, what's the little dongy thing in the back of your throat called?"

"The uvula?" Truly answered.

I put my arm around Truly but said to Brooke and Clay, "I told you she's smart."

"I knew it was a uvula," Theo told Lulu, behind us. "But I like the sound of 'dongy thing.'"

"You would," Lulu said. But then she squeak-laughed. "Dongy thing. That is pretty excellent."

As we started off toward town, I heard Jack asking Truly if she wanted him to carry her books for her.

"Oh, puke," I whispered to Brooke. "What is this, 1958? Carry her books for her?"

"Ha," Brooke said, but not enthusiastically.

Okay. "Plus, she got stitches in her knee; she didn't have her hands both amputated. Get a grip, people." I couldn't tell if Brooke thought that was funny, and was maybe just holding in her laugh. "Too soon?" I asked.

Her older brother always said that last year. He was a big fan of Too Soon, and Brooke is a big fan of her brother. Well, all her siblings. They're like a cult or something, how they stick together and have inside jokes.

But Brooke didn't laugh. She walked away instead, up ahead with Clay and Evangeline. Come on, it was just a joke. I wasn't suggesting we actually amputate Truly's hands. What is wrong with everybody lately?

Both Jack and Clay were practically walking into telephone poles every time Truly blinked. She should just tone it down before she embarrasses herself. Maybe she just doesn't realize. Good thing she has me looking out for her.

Me, full up with *awww* and sympathy.

HAZEL

I DID NOT expect to *like* Brooke. She was supposed to be a shallow plate so I could feel confirmed in my superiority to Truly, who was following Brooke around like a late-afternoon shadow. Or, if Brooke had any spark of intelligence at all, I'd make her realize how meaningless her perfect plastic life is, and she'd be shocked, crushed, her reign as queen of the school doomed to collapse. Either outcome would be fine with me. But then she had to go ahead and be subtly funny. And worse: actually nice. It was messing me up.

If I wanted to be friends with Brooke, what did that make me? The same sad wannabe as every other pathetic girl in the school.

To get over my self-hatred, I had to take action.

So I did something perfect. I was certain of both the righteousness of it and the necessity. Then I wrote this letter

explaining, which of course I have no intention of ever sending. But in case I die suddenly and tragically, this letter will
be found along with the others among my personal effects
and the truth will be discovered. I think the truth remains
important.

> Dear Truly,
>
> Remember when you and I were best friends?
> Ahhh, so many memories. Here's one: last
> month, we mocked how every year at school
> they go on and on about how we should
> keep all our passwords private. Remember?
> You and I were like, what is the deal, here?
> They tell us to trust one another, to turn to
> one another for support. They encourage
> us to be worthy of the trust our friends so
> rightly place in us. But then they add, don't
> tell your friends, even your best friends, your
> e-mail and phone passwords, or your locker
> combinations. Why? Because in fact you can't
> trust anybody. Remember that?
>
> Yeah. Turns out, they have a good point.
>
> They should probably emphasize more the
> trick of don't make your password for your

e-mail and all your social media stuff just be
your locker combination, or, for example,
locker143542, if that happens to be your
locker combination.

It is just too easy for somebody who used
to be your best friend (until you dumped
her) to guess such a thing, Truly, especially
if you already told her (that is, me) your
locker combination. And gave her (me) your
password on a Post-it note.

Because then it is way too easy for that
person, even a very nice person, if she is a
person with any computer skills—a person
like, say, me—to hack into your account and
for example send Brooke a copy of an e-mail
that Natasha sent you today.

I have to admit I was nauseated when I read
that e-mail. It was the one about Henry and
Molly. You must know the one I mean.

I knew Natasha was awful but I was
unprepared for that level of despicableness,
despite the fact that none of her e-mails (all of
which I read, of course) were the slightest bit
interesting or kind.

But after the particular e-mail in question,
even though I am not particularly close
with Henry and I get the sense Molly thinks
I'm weird (she always asks about my hair), I
honestly wanted to go over to Natasha's house
and kick her in the large teeth.

Then I thought of a better plan.

As you may have guessed, Truly, it was the
e-mail about how you act all innocent but
obviously you're scheming to make Clay like
you. She knows you're awkward with people,
just like your brother who has Asperger's and
your sister who has behavior issues. Obviously
social disability runs in your family, so she
is just trying to help you learn how to act
normal.

It was like a clinic, that e-mail; a perfect
machine gun spraying bullets of insult on you
and your brother and your sister, all at once.
I was just about ready to erect the barricades
to fight for you all. Even if they weren't both
so intelligent and interesting, they wouldn't
deserve to be insulted like that, by that
judgmental lemonhead who was just trolling
you, anyway. And I knew where to get backup.

You may be surprised to learn this but I got to know Brooke somewhat intimately, very quickly, three days ago. So I can say with some confidence that I had already gotten some deep insight into Brooke's character. Due to her presence at one of the worst moments of my life (at the death of someone very dear to me; I'm not ready to discuss it) I had learned that Brooke was someone of rare sensitivity and morals.

I knew in my heart that Brooke would want to know what Natasha wrote to you. I was certain that Brooke was someone who would not like one of her friends (that is, Natasha) treating another of her friends (meaning *you*) like that. I also suspected that she would not approve of her supposed friend being nasty about neurological or psychological or learning differences. Not just because her younger brother goes to resource room, where I volunteer after school on Tuesdays, and where he struggles mightily (though of course adorably) let me tell you.

Just generally, too. I think people don't realize what a good person Brooke is. They think she's pretty and cool only. They sell her short, in my opinion.

Since I was certain Natasha would feel worse about whatever Brooke decided to do to her than she would about anything I could do, even kick her in her large, expensive teeth, I realized that the best course of action would be just to alert Brooke. To the facts. No elaboration required. I could stay here in the shadows, unseen, unnoticed as usual. No suggestions of how to handle what she read, no parameters of punishment. Just let Brooke see the e-mail from Natasha to you, and Brooke could decide what was required as a response. I had an extremely strong feeling that Brooke would want to take some action to punish Natasha for what she had written.

And I guess I was right.

As I tend to be.

BROOKE

WAIT, SERIOUSLY?

Is she kidding me?

Who does something like that, put down somebody's sibs? And why? Just to make the friend feel crappy or embarrassed about herself—and her *family*?

Not that she should even feel embarrassed because come on, we all have our issues, you get whatever brain or body you get *and* whatever sibs, too. My little brother Corey is a monster and a half, total pain in my butt, but if somebody said something down-putting about him? My door is slammed shut to you from then on, ex-friend.

But that was so obviously what Natasha's intention was, and worse: to offhandedly mention Truly's brother's and sister's issues, in order to intimidate Truly and make her think she is *less than*, make her think she is awkward and being judged harshly. By *us*.

Making me and Evangeline and Clay and Lulu and Jack

seem like we would all privately think less of Truly because of whatever struggles her family has.

Screw you, Natasha. No.

Screw you for saying anything mean about two kids I don't even know, who might or even might not have problems. None of my business, but if they do have stuff to deal with, more power to them. They're probably working harder than any of us just to get through the day. But screw you even more for thinking you speak for me or anybody else in putting them down.

You think you're going to act like that, all conniving and passive-aggressively abusive, and then still have friends when the day is done?

No.

Just, no.

TRULY

I DON'T KNOW what happened today but because of something, something I have to figure happened online or last night or I don't know when or where—Natasha got kicked out of the Popular Table.

Brooke was sitting where Natasha usually sits when Natasha and I walked into the cafeteria. I was walking around to where I usually (well, for the past two weeks) sit. So I didn't hear exactly what they said, very quietly, to each other. The thing I did hear was Brooke saying to Natasha, "Why don't *you* stop pretending to be all innocent?"

Natasha glared at Brooke for a second and then at Clay and me for a bunch more. Clay got very interested in his sandwich. I stayed still and small.

"Maybe find somewhere else to sit," Brooke said to Natasha.

Natasha smiled tensely. "Brooke . . ."

"I'm serious," Brooke said.

Natasha stormed away, tossing her full lunch bag in the trash as she went.

My stomach was in such a knot I couldn't open my own lunch bag, either. I just sat there, trying not to move until Brooke and Clay finished eating their lunches. I tossed my untouched lunch into the garbage next to Natasha's and followed everybody else out to the playground.

I started biting my fingernails again. Mom hasn't noticed yet but I'm sure she will very soon. I'm down to the nubs. It's bad. Brooke has such pretty hands she could be in nail polish ads. I have to get this under control.

But all I have to do now is start wondering if I am the next one to be kicked out of the Popular Table, especially since Natasha is the one who brought me in and was trying to be my protector against everybody else I don't know very well, and apparently I keep messing up, and within the minute I am gnawing at my cuticles like they're the only food in a famine.

NATASHA

THEY DUMPED ME. Just like that. No warning, no gradual growing apart. They were my best friends in the world, my sisters, my twins, my future bridesmaids at my wedding, the only people on earth I told my darkest secrets to. Brooke, Lulu, Evangeline—the girls I dressed up with in matching costumes last Halloween. Also just all alike on random days, for fun, because we're such dorks together. These were the girls who totally had my back when Clay and I broke up. Especially Brooke.

Or so I thought.

But as of lunch today, that was all abruptly in the past. I walked into the cafeteria at 11:20 this morning without a clue and headed straight toward our table. But I didn't even get to sit down at it.

Walking out of the cafeteria afterward I wasn't even mad yet. I was just thinking *I will never sit at our table ever again.* Nobody gets invited back in once they're kicked out.

I should know, I was thinking, since I'm the one who made that rule, last May, when Marilicia was kicked out. She deserved it, for being such a damp sponge. She didn't have to be with us, if she thought it was so lame to dress alike for the field trip. Everybody else thought it was a good idea. She didn't need to dis me like that. Everybody agreed. I don't care that she hates me. She does, she's obvious about it. Tough. It was her own fault, and she can go live her sad little life with the other weirdos at the extreme freak table.

But that's not me. I'm no damp sponge. What did I even do? Did I do one foul thing, ever, to Brooke? I mean that she could possibly know about? Seriously—what? Went out with Clay? She said it was fine with her. I have the texts to prove it.

That's when it hit me: even though it was Brooke who did all the talking there at the table today, of course, in her typical calm measured Brooke way, I realized by the time I got to the library with the other outcast losers that it must have been sweet downcast-eyed Truly behind whatever happened.

She must have somehow turned Brooke against me. Maybe as revenge for supposedly, in her words, "dumping" her in sixth grade? Truly is a very patient person, so maybe. Maybe she has been waiting and plotting all this time to, like, give me a taste of my own medicine, make me feel how she must have felt when I unfriended her. But that is so unfair, to turn my best friend against me.

All my friends.

For revenge about something that happened when we were, what? Eleven? Are you kidding me?

Fine, then, I decided, plopping down my books on the library table. That's what she wants? To take me on? Good. Bring it.

I sat there at the front library table perfectly straight and tall like my father always says I should. For the first time it felt good to be straight and tall, because I was buzzing with energy. Tall and strong not like a telephone pole for once but like a badass. As Daddy says, I don't have to shrink down and try to take up less space. I don't have to hide what I am. I'm tall like him, so good. Take charge. I'll never look adorable like Truly, my petite mother has pointed out more than once, and trying only makes me look ridiculous.

Maybe they dumped me because I'm too tall? No, Evangeline is just as tall. The pimples on my forehead? I am doing everything possible to get rid of them. Am I just not pretty enough? I work so hard at being pretty, it's the only hobby I have time for. And nice. Nice, nice, nice, and pretty, my hair smoother, my skin clearer, my clothes perfect. I'm worn-out but it's never enough.

Be yourself, the adults always say. Yeah, right: myself. Which is who, exactly? Myself is some gawky stranger. I don't even know her. Myself is the girl who just got dumped by her best friends. Why would I want to be her?

Mom would probably be like, yeah, well, you must've done something wrong if all your friends hate you. If I told her this happened. Which, ha, no.

Fine. I'll be who I really am: tall, strong, and independent, like Daddy tells me to be. Like all his willowy ditz girl-friends. Well, they're all tall, at least.

Brooke thinks Truly is so sweet and innocent, but she doesn't know Truly like I do. Thanks to me, Brooke and Truly are whispering in the halls, cracking each other up, passing notes. Three weeks, less, and those two are tight as new jeans.

And who's left out now? Me.

But not for long.

What really pisses me off is, I tried to be nice to Truly. Help her. Bring her into the popular crowd, like she so obviously wanted to be. She dumped her green-haired best bud in one hot heartbeat when I just mentioned she could sit with us once at lunch.

What kind of person does *that*?

That's what I should've said to Brooke, when she said to me, what kind of person does what you did, Natasha?

Does what? Is all I came up with, and she wouldn't explain.

That's what I would say to a jury: what kind of person dumps her best friend the second she gets a chance to sit at the Popular Table? Right? Boom! They'd all agree. What kind of person? A shallow, selfish person is the answer. I was just trying to be nice to her, give her exactly what she wanted, and this is how I'm repaid? She barges in and takes my seat at the table the way my frigging temporary step-father took my dad's seat at our kitchen table back when? And Truly of all people knows—she had to know—how that would feel to me. She was my best friend during that whole crap-storm—and now she's decided to make that run on repeat in my actual life?

The more I thought about it, the angrier I got at her. It was, like, diabolical, what she had done to me. She totally plotted the perfect revenge for sixth grade. It wasn't my fault Truly still wanted to play with her plastic horses and imagine we were runaways in the Wild West when I wanted to figure out how to do a smoky eye. We grew apart. It happens.

Maybe, horrifyingly, my mom was right: the whole time we were best friends, Truly thought she was better than me. Better at school, cuter, thinner, prettier, more cheerful, with her perfect little family of five plus cute little dog, while my family was such a mess, then. There in their perfect house with the neat hall closet with twenty extra rolls of toilet paper and twenty more of paper towels all lined up on the shelf. That closet totally killed me. Anytime these past few years I was tempted to be friends with Truly again, I'd just picture that closet with all the spare rolls of toilet paper and paper towels and, no. No way. They'd never run short of anything and have to use the napkins from the bottom of the takeout bag. They always had more than enough, at Truly's. They didn't even have to finish the cereal. They didn't have to eat the crumbs that clog up the milk in the bowl because don't be a spoiled brat, it's still food as my dad says. "Just toss that," Truly's dad told me one time on a sleepover. "You can open a fresh box." I'll never forget that. *Open a fresh box.*

So Truly pitied me.

I always thought Mom was the mean one. But at least she tells the truth. If she thinks I look bad, she says so. If my laugh sounds like a hyena's, Mom lets me know. Truly acts like she thinks I'm great, but maybe that's way meaner, really, if she actually hates me deep down.

She just sat there today at lunch, eyes down, with her long straight hair and her perfect flat chest, tiny Truly the new pet project of my best friend Brooke.

My best friend.

Truly obviously told Brooke that I mentioned to her not to act all innocent about how much she was flirting with Clay. So what? My own mom says stuff like that to me all the time: *Don't act so innocent, Miss Natasha, I'm on to you!*

Anyway, I was trying to help Truly out! Oh, no, my advice hurt her feelings? Poor little snowflake. Like she is the only person on earth to ever have her feelings hurt, like hurt feelings are nuclear war.

Actually, it's the same thing she did with that girl Hazel's note. Turned it around so she was the victim: you hurt some poor innocent girl by randomly dumping her? Call 911!!!! *You've* been assaulted!

And I fell for it. I thought I was playing Truly—but all the time she was using me. As soon as her position at the Popular Table was set, boom! Good-bye, me.

Truly was obviously sending me a message that she can take anything of mine—my mom braiding her hair instead of mine in the middle of the night, my place at the lunch table, Clay's attention, Brooke's friendship. And then pretend she had no plan, no evil intent. All sweetness and light, our Truly.

But I see through her now. Like she's made of glass.

CLAY

From: Clay4Ever@gmail.com
To: JTEverett@Stanford.edu

Hey JT—

How's college life?

We went to the waffle cart in the park today, for "family time." I know. Sorry. We fully missed you.

Especially because of this guy ahead of us in line. He was kind of a chunky guy. Not in consistency but in shape. Kept hiking up his pants because they were sliding down the bottom slope of his belly. The guy was looking down the whole time, like if he didn't see people, nobody would see him, either.

I was like, I feel you, Chunky Guy. You and me, dude. Because okay, I'll tell you but DON'T SAY ANYTHING TO MOM.

We were all hanging out at Evangeline's last night, got pizza and watched this ridiculous movie in her basement. But—remember Natasha? The one you were like, *oh man, she's in your grade? Holy.* Yeah. Well I went out with her briefly a few weeks ago. Cuz I'm all that. Uh-huh. But you know the crazy-hot scale? She's way over the line into crazy-land. So I had to end that.

Not because of Brooke so don't even go there.

Anyway, Natasha wasn't invited and it was a whole thing. They're in some fight, the girls, and they didn't want her over. None of my business, whatever. They're always in a fight and then crying and hugging and then not talking to each other and then hugging it out again and they all tell me stuff but even though I'm like, *yeah wow that sucks*, honestly what I'm thinking about is *man I wish I had some pizza.*

Natasha texted me like 50 times while I was
at Evangeline's until I finally just turned off
my phone. Then this morning she was still at
it until finally I was like WHAT?

And she texted back: *Fine, forget it.*

And then nothing.

Which, good, right? Done.

So when I felt my phone buzzing in my pocket
while I was waiting in that line I was like,
leave me alone, would you please? Because if
I answered she'd yell at me, and Mom would
hear, and—exactly. Then it's a Thing.

Especially because don't tell them this either
I failed another algebra quiz. Actually failed
this time, though. 62. DO NOT REPEAT
THAT. Seriously. They'd string me up. They
would've had my privates in the blender for
the 78 if they knew, and you even admitted
that. They'd boot me out of the family for this.

Anyway, the chunky guy got to the front of
the line right about then.

The girl in the cart was like, *How can I help you?*

He smiled up at her sadly, like, honey, there is really no helping me at this point, and ordered a waffle with bacon and syrup and all the fixings on it. But he didn't come out and say "I'll have the Top-o'-the-Morning Waffle even though it is three o'clock in the afternoon and it is pure cruelty to make a grown man say Top-o'-the-Morning Waffle as if my humiliation at being about to eat a waffle loaded up with bacon, syrup, potatoes, eggs, and cheese is insufficient to kill me right here."

Nope.

What he said was, *I'll have some of that . . . uh . . . bacon situation.*

Like: yeah not sure what exactly is gonna happen here but whatever, I'm a man. I'll handle whatever comes. I'm a boss. I can deal. I'll have some of that, uh, bacon situation.

Right? Don't you just LOVE that guy?

He killed it. Faced down his potential shame with the awesome evasive power of a master ninja. *Some of that, uh, bacon situation.* YES.

I so wish you'd been there. Mom and Dad had no clue what happened. Even after I told them, they didn't get why I was cracking up and so stoked. But you would've been all over that. I know you would've.

Just, perfection. Right? I wanted to shake that guy's hand, but I didn't want to bother him. Respect. He is the man.

I am so going to use that line anytime life craps on me. Some of this, uh, Natasha situation. Some of this, uh, girl situation. Some of this listen to music and play Xbox instead of doing my homework situation.

That guy is my new hero. Sorry, JT. Shuffle your feet, he took your seat.

I'll have some of that . . . bacon situation.

Sometimes I miss you a little.

TRULY

MY PARENTS LOOK at each other with worried faces every time they check the stitches. At least they let me go to the sleepover at Evangeline's this weekend, even if they were the first to pick up this morning. They keep telling me I need to keep my leg elevated because of the swelling. But I can't keep it elevated.

It's my leg.

All the basic jobs of a leg involve being down.

And it is still oozing. I can't even look at it, it's so gross. My mother has to change the bandage on it. I'm not officially supposed to have a bandage on it anymore, because it needs to get air to dry out. But then I end up looking at it, which makes me all woozy.

I'm going to have a scar, Dad said. Forcing a smile, he assured me that scars give you character.

Now of course my sister Molly wants a scar.

Tonight she had a whole temper tantrum about how it's

not fair that I get to have a scar and character, if she doesn't. And it's not fair that I get two chairs at the dinner table, one for my leg and one for the rest of me. Eventually Dad brought over his desk chair for Molly to prop under her perfectly fine leg. Just to settle her down.

The only thing that stings more than my knee-gash is how Natasha keeps glaring at me. Brooke says not to worry, that Natasha is just moody and has to chill for a while. Better to not engage.

It's hard not to engage when every time I say anything in school she is there, slicing her narrow eyes away from me. I get the feeling she thinks it's somehow my fault, this fight she had with Brooke. Brooke doesn't want to discuss it. She just said, "Well, after that stuff Natasha said . . ."

"What stuff?" I asked.

Brooke closed her eyes slowly. "You're right."

"About what?"

"No," Brooke said. "My bad. I shouldn't have even . . . I respect that you don't want to talk about it."

"Okay," I said, though I did want to talk about it.

"But I'm glad you reached out to me," Brooke whispered. "It was the right thing to do."

"I did?"

"I know you didn't ask for help. I just, anyway. Moving on, right?"

"Right," I said. "So anyway, about, I mean, I don't know what Natasha—"

"I don't either," Brooke interrupted. "But you know what?

There comes a point where you have to just say, no way."

"I guess," I said, though honestly, what?

But then we had to rush to get to eighth period.

Maybe something happened after I got picked up at five thirty at the pizza place last week? Or maybe something to do with Clay? Because he and Brooke are very close and I know Natasha dumped him. He apparently had terrible breath and was a too-forceful kisser, which sounds really awful. But maybe he just didn't know how to kiss well, because maybe it was his first kiss and didn't realize. And maybe he just forgot to brush his teeth. That could happen to a person, especially one as laid-back as Clay. And maybe Natasha was too harsh about it and Brooke defended him.

But if that's not it, maybe there's some unwritten rule Natasha violated. If I don't know the rule, I could do the same unforgivable thing by accident. So it's not purely generosity and wanting to help my friends make up, if I'm honest. There's also the selfish question of: what did she *do*?

Maybe it was flirting?

Natasha told me that everybody was talking about how flirtatious I've been. I know they all say that about her. Maybe that's what she did wrong?

And so maybe I'm next to get kicked out?

Mom noticed my nails. I knew she would. I'm covered in Bite No More and Band-Aids now. I look like I'm heading home from war.

Last night after the boys left Evangeline's house, Lulu

asked me who I like, Clay or Jack. I don't really have a good answer to that other than gobble up my own fingers. I forced them into my pockets and shrugged instead.

Brooke said, "Truly's very private about that stuff."

But that's not really why I'm not saying who I like.

I barely know Clay, but I think he's in love with Brooke. They talk in almost a private language, a rhythm nobody else can get in on, like they're playing double Dutch but everybody else at best can do regular jump rope. They seem like they're already a couple even though they don't realize it.

And about Jack: he is very sweet, and distractingly good-looking. But I can't even see him without thinking of my knee innards. Also he scares me a little. He picked me up and carried me to the nurse's office after I got hurt. He held me like I was a pile of summer laundry.

I know I am small for my age, but I weigh more than a pile of cotton sundresses. My own father hasn't picked me up since I turned nine. Jack might be bigger than my *dad*. Which feels not okay.

Plus, while he was holding me in the nurse's office, I think a small amount of nose goo may have gotten onto Jack's shirt. From my nose. So there's that to be embarrassed about, too.

But mostly, I just don't actually have a crush on anybody. I'm not even fully sure how a crush would feel. I don't want to admit that, though, because my new friends are mature. They talk a lot about crushes. I need to stop imagining shape-shifting powers and tiny worlds with magical elves living in them all the time. I am trying to be more interested in crushes than in math, wars, and racial injustice. I am thirteen years old. Time to grow up.

If my new friends knew I didn't have a crush on anybody yet, maybe they would think I am too babyish to hang with them, and make me go back to my old table. But I can't, because everybody at that table hates me now. So I would be completely alone, which would be so awful I can't even think about it without eating up my fingers despite the poison Mom coated them with.

This morning after we blew down the air mattresses at Evangeline's, we worked a little on the History Day project. When Evangeline got up to go to the bathroom, she left her computer open. Lulu posted, as if she were Evangeline: "My name is Evangeline and I like smelling basketballs, library books, and poop."

She and Brooke thought that was a riot. Brooke added, "And my best friend is Brooke, who is the BEST person in the world!"

"Won't she know it's you, then?" I asked, which cracked them up more. They couldn't believe I didn't have some of the apps they all have. I figured it was okay to download them because they were free and I am over thirteen now. It's all just easy goofy fun. Everybody chiming in I LOVE YOU! And YOU WATCH THAT TOO? And *How are you SO PRETTY?* And *OMG that was so funny lolz.*

So I was fairly sure these other apps and social sites would be fine with Mom, too. Everybody has them. Facebook is pretty done, now that everybody's parents are on it. It's boring anyway. Not that we stay off it, hahahaha. But still. We don't want our parents all up in our business. Apparently.

When Evangeline got back, they were still laughing. She immediately checked and saw what they'd done. She commented under it, "#smellygirls #yolo" and everybody rushed to like that from our phones. Then we took lots of pictures including selfies. We posted them on various sites and liked them, especially the ones where we made funny faces or kissed each other's cheeks while looking at the camera. We entered them into contests for how cute are we and then voted for ourselves a lot. We basically alternated between teasing, saying, We are such losers! And then saying how pretty we were. And how much we love each other.

I was kind of catching on, it felt like. We were literally falling down laughing. So we decided to make up a hilarious dance routine to the song we have to do in chorus, which I will now never be able to sing with a straight face again, especially the verse where we all pretended to be attacking each other with cans of hair spray and Windex. OMG we thought we were the best comedy team ever. We got close to nothing done on the Benedict Arnold project but #yolo and also, my face was sore from so much laughing.

So now I'm lying here in bed, clicking through pictures and apps. I've gotten forty-seven "likes" on average on my posted photos. The one where I'm looking back over my shoulder the way Evangeline said I should, I'm up to seventy-nine. Eighty. Eighty-three. I don't even know a lot of those people. A lot of them are boys. I haven't really been friends with boys since about kindergarten, until now. I have more friends—well, "friends"—every day. I keep checking the number of friends and likes I have, and they both keep going up up up.

HAZEL

So, Truly,

I won't be sending you this letter, nor any of the others I've written to you. At least, not yet. Not for a while. I just write them to stop myself from accidentally calling you when I have an interesting thought and who else can I really talk with about those?

Like here's a quote I just found, in my wanderings on the Internet, and I almost posted it on your wall before I remembered that social media is stupid and also I'm not talking to you:

We shall not cease from exploration, and the end of all our exploring will be to arrive where we started and know the place for the first time.   —*T. S. Eliot*

I am not completely positive what that quote means, but it definitely feels meaningful. What a piece of crap journey, though, if you just end up where you started, right? And you're like, oh, wait, I'm here again? After all this journeying I just did, and all these blisters? You'd have to wonder what kind of idiot you are at that point. You could have stayed home and watched a full season of some good show. But still. It's a deep thought.

Maybe I will post it as my status update and see if I get one one-hundredth of how many likes you get every time you post a photo of yourself puckering your lips. I doubt it.

And T. S. Eliot was a great poet or writer or, possibly, dancer. Maybe he was just a weary traveler with poor map skills and a gift for quotable sentences. But did he post kissy-face photos of himself on multiple Web sites? I doubt it.

Meanwhile, it turns out your Facebook and Instagram and Snapchat and all those kinds of accounts are just as easy to gain access to as your e-mail. Especially because you use the same password and user name for all of them. Maybe I'll post the T. S. Eliot quote as *your* status update. See how your new buddies react to *that*.

I have of course changed all of my user names and passwords since that day when you and I made them up together and wrote them down on those Post-it notes at your house, and decided we'd hide them in our jewelry boxes so nobody would ever find them. We thought we were being so sly, so safe.

I recently buried the jewelry box that was the twin to yours, Truly, the one you and I both had with the tiny ballerina twirling inside, personifying all a little girl's dreams. I buried it, along with my dead bird who was not who I thought he was, either. Pretty powerful symbolism, if you ask me.

I am a big fan of symbolism. Also, righteousness.

I may use the symbolism of my dead bird and/or those jewelry boxes in the writing project/personal reflection for English homework. Either that or my grandmother's life story, which I believe will bring her solace in the hospital. I will dedicate that story to her, if I choose to go that route. My father will appreciate the gesture, I think, but I may do it anyway.

I know many of the details of my grandmother's life, and feel I might be able to conjure the rest from intuition and imagination. Even though Grandee is a raging bigot and hates all children and most animals, she has good qualities. For instance: she knows how to wear a scarf. Few women do. I've heard her mention this fact often over the years to my mother, who apparently does not know how to wear a scarf. Maybe Grandee will leave her scarf collection to me in her will, if she ever dies.

On the other hand, I may go with the other story idea, with the dead bird and the murdered friendship. I have a different dedication in mind for that one. (Spoiler alert: it's you.)

If my dreams somehow don't come true and I can't be a humanitarian or a movie star and travel the world glamorously, I still plan to live life to the hilt. New ambitions I am cultivating include writer and computer

hacker, or possibly a T. S. Eliot scholar. So
the future is wide open.

Even the past is wide open.

I opened your account, Truly, and held my
hands above the keyboard high, the way you
do. I fluttered my eyelids like you do yours.
And then I posted your photo, your words
which I was making up, all as if I were you. I
felt for the first time ever absolutely adorable.
It was a rush. Fun. So I kept going.

NATASHA

TRULY DIDN'T HAVE to post that photo to show who was invited to her house tomorrow. She didn't need to post what their plans were. She just didn't need to post anything about it at all.

If she was going to post it, maybe she could have proofread it.

Wait. Truly *always* proofreads. She proofreads to-do lists. When she grows up, for her job she could be AutoCorrect.

Which means there was no mistake. She did it on purpose.

She posted a picture of me, her, Brooke, Evangeline, and Lulu (with my eyes half-closed—thanks) and tagged us all. She titled it: *Can't wait for 2morrow!!! History will be made (Up)!!!*

And then ten minutes later, as a comment, she wrote: *Oops!*

And then she posted a new picture, except this time one without me in it.

She commented under that: *Shoot me now I am such an idiot* 😳 A good suggestion. Followed by a correct fact.

I "liked" the *shoot me now I am such an idiot* comment. That is the only thing of hers I "liked." In fact I went through everything else of hers that I had ever "liked" and "unliked" it all. Every last thing.

Before I even finished unliking everything, Truly had taken down the posts. But I had screen shots. Nothing goes away without leaving a stain, as my mom has said.

People think I'm mean. I know they do. Fine. Maybe I am. Or maybe, like Daddy says, it's just that I'm tall and have blonde hair (whatever, dirty blonde), so they're jealous.

That day Daddy said they were all probably jealous of my hair was one of the best days of my life.

All my friends had been acting obnoxious to me for like a week last year, and I was starting to kind of buckle under. Daddy took me to a diner that Saturday just the two of us for a change, no bimbo, and he was like *Would you stop moping around what is the matter with you?* So I was like, *My friends are all, like, picking on me lately* and he was like, *Well, they're probably just jealous that's how women act when they're jealous.* And I was like, *Yeah right jealous of what?* Because I was feeling like crap. But Daddy was like, *I don't know—maybe that you're a blonde and dress hot so the boys can't keep their eyes off you?*

When I got home and told Mom, I thought she'd say yeah well your father is an idiot, but she didn't. She said, yeah that's probably true and then went out back to smoke a cigarette.

It changed everything for me. I went from mopey and depressed to on top of the world, just like that. Yeah, they're just jealous of my hair! I had to be patient with them, and forgiving. I was almost in shock that there was something good enough about me that people would be jealous of it. Usually Mom is all about why am I so annoyingly LARGE.

The next day she was back to *Didn't I tell you to tone down what you're wearing?* And, *your father is a sexist jerk who should not be making gross comments about what women are like because most women are not awful jealous toddlers like he imagines.* But she had let the secret out: She thought my hair was jealousy-worthy and I looked hot in what I wore.

I felt much more confident after that. Mom sounds mean sometimes, but I know inside she's a total softie. The most popular celebrities are always that type: tough on the outside, but sweet deep down.

Truly is the opposite.

People think I'm all tough and she's all sweet. But the fact is, we're both the opposite *on the inside. Where it counts.* I would never do something as mean as what (supposedly) sweet innocent Truly did, posting stuff and then taking it back, just to publicly humiliate me.

I really wouldn't.

And Brooke can believe that or not. It's so hard to tell what she thinks. I am so done trying. There's nothing more I can do to convince her.

Or at least nothing I can think of yet.

Maybe I should just go ahead and post that picture of me and Brooke and Lulu all jumping up in the air together last June. That is such a fun one. We were having such a blast that day. Where was Evangeline? At that basketball camp maybe? And of course Truly didn't exist, then.

Or maybe I should post the one with me and Brooke sticking out our tongues. That might be my best photo of all time. Mom said she can't stand how grown-up I look in that one. It's why she didn't want me to post it right away, even though she said I look really pretty in it, way prettier than Brooke even.

Clay thought I looked good that night, too. He must have. That was the night he asked me out, and then later we kissed behind the couch in his basement.

There was a good shot of me and Clay, from that same night. Brooke took that one and sent it to me. For two days I considered making it my profile picture. When he dumped me, I was so relieved I hadn't posted it anywhere. I deleted it from my phone and my computer, even my hard drive. Now I almost wish I hadn't. Sometimes my eyes in pictures look like somebody just jumped out from behind something and shouted *boo* but not in that picture, the one with Clay in front of his couch. I looked nice and relaxed.

But now it's gone. Kind of sad how such an important and pretty moment of a person's life can be deleted like it never happened.

I guess that's what Brooke wants to do to me, now. Delete

me. How is Truly not being deleted instead, though, if being "mean" is the hugest crime in the world? I so don't get it. I did *nothing* to her. I offered a little advice is *all*. And what did *she* just do?

Yeah. She just posted that I was part of a group of my apparently former best friends and then, *lol, jk, obviously YOU are not invited, Natasha! Just thought the world should know that!*

How is that not WAY meaner than any mean thing I ever did? To anybody?

Oh well. Great, whatever. As Brooke would say. Because nothing ever freaking bothers her.

Or me.

Anymore.

Seriously, I am so over everything. I told Brooke my side of it today, again, and there's nothing more for me to do now I guess. I don't even know if I'm still in the Benedict Arnold play anymore. Am I supposed to do my own project all of a sudden, now? I don't even know. It sucks. When Mom stopped being friends with Truly's mom, she just avoided her. But how am I supposed to deal? I am still in a History Day group with all my ex-friends. I still sit next to them in assigned seats in class. I can't escape, ever.

Well, neither can they. They can kick me out of their table but I don't think they actually can kick me out of a History Day group once it's been okayed.

I pulled up the picture of me and Brooke again. The one with the tongues. We really do look like we could be sisters.

At least cousins. Really cute cousins. Or, like, best friends. So happy.

And Truly is nowhere to be seen.

I think maybe I will just go ahead and post that one. What's Brooke going to do, untag herself? Unfriend me online, too, because I posted a photo where she looks super pretty?

(Even if maybe I look for once a tiny bit possibly prettier?)

CLAY

Natasha:

Okay, okay. I'm answering.
Chill. Seriously. Don't text me fifty times.
Hold up.

No not everybody hates you.
I doubt anybody hates you.

I like you fine, but here's the thing: I just don't
want to be going out with anybody right now. It
was better anyway when we used to be friends
and we would talk about actual stuff. Like how
you want to be a scientist. Was it a botanist?
Biologist? Instead of whether I like you, or
Brooke likes you, or if I like Truly.

I hardly even know Truly. She seems nice enough. That. Is. All.
Okay?

And yeah, okay, I agree, that sucked of them to kick you out of the lunch table. And it was mean for Truly to post who was coming over and include you and then dump you.

So maybe she's not that nice. I don't know. Don't care. Gotta go play some Xbox and blow off algebra. #YOLO.

My advice? Just step back a bit. Chill. Be nice and smart like I know you are deep down, and stuff will work itself out with the whole friend . . . situation.

BROOKE

WE WENT OVER to Truly's house to work on the History Day project, since we have done approximately zero on it so far and History Day is a week from Friday. We took the school bus there. I sat with Lulu, who was texting with her dad to let him know where we were heading and what time she'd be home. He keeps pretty close tabs on her.

"All good?" I asked her.

She nodded. "You?"

"Great." Lulu started playing some game of shooting zombies on her phone. "Keeping the world safe for us?" I asked her.

"You know it," Lulu muttered. "I'm just . . . hold on." Lulu jerked her phone around, then dropped it into her lap. "Sorry, zombies won."

"Story of my life," I said. The bus whined to a stop.

"This is us," Truly said. We followed her off.

Walking up the street, we passed Big Pond. It freezes over

in the winter sometimes, but a few years ago some kids went out to mess around on the ice and fell through because it wasn't solid enough yet, so they had to get rescued. They all ended up in the hospital, and one kid's finger had such bad frostbite it got partially amputated. The kid has nine and a half fingers now. My older brother Otto saw it.

Anyway, since then, nobody is allowed to skate on Big Pond or go too near it even in the summer. A bunch of parents keep trying to get the town to build a fence around it but so far, no. It's just there, open and waiting for more kids to fall in and get parts of their fingers chopped off.

You're supposed to touch each finger with your thumbs as you pass it, is the tradition. Or superstition. I did it, of course, and watched Lulu do it, beside me. Up ahead of us, Truly and Evangeline were tapping away, without probably even thinking of what they were doing. Everybody just does it.

After we passed, Lulu whispered, "That was pretty crappy, don't you think?"

"What was? The finger chopping?"

"Ew," Lulu squealed. "No! Not that! How Truly tagged Natasha and then untagged her! Natasha's eyes were all red this morning. Did you see?"

"Yeah," I whispered back. "Truly took both posts down right away, as soon as we told her to."

"Still."

"I know."

When we got into her house, Truly kicked her shoes off with opposite toes on the heels. So we all did the same. Some houses are shoes off, some are shoes on. You never know until you go in.

Her house is pretty normal, more like mine and the rest of ours than like Hazel's. I'd been wondering, since she used to be really close with Hazel. It's funny they were friends, because Hazel seems so much wackier than Truly. But maybe I just haven't gotten to know Truly yet. Maybe everybody is nuttier, down deep, than anybody realizes.

Even those of us who seem full-on normal might be secretly odd.

I keep thinking about that day at Hazel's. It wasn't boring, that's for sure. I usually just do the activities in front of me and don't think that much. I just basically have fun with whatever I'm doing. But since that day at Hazel's I've been kind of *thinking* more. Bird flu, I guess. Hahahaha. Too soon?

"Hi, True!" her mom called, coming toward us from the kitchen. "You all must be . . ."

We introduced ourselves. Truly's mom had kind of a gravelly voice, too, like Truly's. She promised to keep Molly and Henry out of our hair while we worked on our project. I had kind of been hoping to meet them, actually.

Oh, well.

We followed Truly into the family room. There were two couches and a chair, all covered in blue plaids and swirls. Contrasting pillows, loads of them, leaned against all the arms. No papers or piles of stuff crowded around, like in my house, where there's sports equipment and books everywhere.

There was a navy blue rug in the middle of the room, with the front legs of both couches and the chair on it. A big square wood coffee table in the middle of the rug held two stacks of plain white paper, a jar full of markers all from the same set, a matching jar full of sharpened colored pencils, and a glass bowl full of M&M's. Everything looked brand-new, just bought. It seemed more like a photo of a family room in a catalog than an actual room.

"This is awesome," Lulu said.

"Thanks," Truly answered. "My mom likes when people come over."

"Lucky you," Lulu said.

Nobody said anything. I wasn't sure if Truly even knew about Lulu's mom.

"I guess," Truly whispered eventually.

We sat down to work on Benedict Arnold and also the M&M's. Truly was reviewing the story with us about how Benedict Arnold had betrayed George Washington. It played out, she said, over breakfast at Benedict and Peggy's house, when George Washington surprised them a day earlier than expected, exactly at the moment he was trying to turn over West Point to the British.

We all agreed that was awesome, and that we should have breakfast foods as props.

"So what about Natasha?" Evangeline asked, arms crossed. "Is she still my wife?"

Lulu chewed on a marker cap. Probably Truly's mom bought the fresh pack of markers, a jumbo pack, special for

this project. What were we going to use all those markers for?
"Ms. Canuto said we can't change the groups," Lulu said.

They all looked at me. "So she'll be in it," I said. "Whatever."

"Do I still have to be the slimy French guy who gets Benedict to betray his country?" Lulu asked.

"Yeah," Evangeline said. "And you have to have an affair with Natasha."

"I have an affair with her?" Lulu asked. "While she's married to you?"

Truly started to shrug but changed to a nod. "I think so, yes."

"I suck!" Lulu squeaked.

"Yeah, you're pretty evil," Evangeline agreed, scooping a handful of M&M's into her mouth.

"I think Natasha is really the evil one," Truly said.

Truly's mom came in right then with a plate of homemade cookies and one of dried fruit. "Why is Natasha evil?" she asked.

"Oh, not actual Natasha," Lulu said agreeably. "Her character in our play."

"Peggy Shippen," Truly explained. "Benedict Arnold's wife. She's the evil mastermind, I think."

"Truly, may I speak privately with you?" her mom asked.

Truly stood up quickly and followed her mom out of the room. And didn't come back for a long time. A boy came in, his hair spiking out in every direction.

"Hi," I said to him.

"I'm not interfering in your project," he said, staring into my eyes without blinking.

"We're not doing anything, really," Evangeline said. "Truly's the only one who's done any research, so we're basically just looking at cookies."

"You're supposed to be doing a project on Benedict Arnold," he said. "I know a lot about Benedict Arnold."

I held up a few blank sheets of paper. "Us, too."

"You do?"

"No," I said, feeling bad, not meaning to tease him. "Practically nothing."

"You were joking," he said.

"It's hard to tell," Evangeline said. "Brooke has a terrible sense of humor."

"So do I," the boy said as I threw a bunch of papers at Evangeline.

"Think we can start on these cookies?" Evangeline asked him. "I'm starving."

"Yes, you can," he said. We each grabbed some. He stood in the doorway watching. I held out the plate to him. "Those are for you," he said. "Truly's friends."

"You're her friend, too," I said. "Aren't you?"

"No," he said. "I'm her brother. Henry."

"Is she in trouble, you think?" Lulu whispered to him. "Did we do something wrong?"

"Truly doesn't get in trouble," Henry said.

"They're good," I said. "These cookies."

"They have a lot of butter in them," Henry said. "If you

have questions on Benedict Arnold I could answer them. Or on butter. I know a lot of facts."

"Cool," I said. "Thanks, Henry. Any facts you've got would help because . . ."

Truly came back in, then, her eyes on her feet as they crossed onto the rug. Their mom called Henry into the kitchen. I wasn't sure if she was Mrs. Gonzales or Ms. Something Else or a first name mom. She hadn't said.

"See ya," I said to Henry's back. He didn't respond.

"Everything okay?" Evangeline whispered to Truly.

"Natasha's mom just called," Truly whispered.

"Oh," Lulu said.

"My mom thinks I . . . she doesn't believe me, that I didn't post that stuff saying who was coming, leaving Natasha out. And she thinks I was saying that Natasha is evil. She thinks I was being purposely cruel to Natasha, now."

"Maybe Natasha deserved it," Evangeline said. "What you did online. You don't have to make excuses. Natasha does a lot of—"

"But I *didn't* post it," Truly said. Her eyeballs were practically jumping out of her skull.

We looked at one another briefly. Why was she insisting on that obvious lie? Denial was only making it worse. People should just own what they do, and who they are. That's what Margot says, and even though she was torturing me that I should admit to liking Clay at the time she said that, I still think she was right. Own it. Mom and Dad failed at owning our store. Not their fault—they tried adding coffee and dad's homemade muffins and late night hours on Thursdays with author readings, but still it's hard to make a bookstore stay in business these days. So they owned up to it not working out and they're trying to sell, start over, try something else. No shame in that. A lot to respect, in fact.

The reason I was keeping it to myself was for privacy, not shame.

"Maybe you posted it by accident on purpose," I said to Truly.

"But I didn't," Truly said.

Why would she keep denying it when we all saw it? If my friends asked about my parents, I wouldn't flat-out deny it. I wouldn't lie. Why would I? They'll all find out eventually anyway. The truth always comes out. Doesn't it?

"You took them down," Lulu said to Truly.

"As soon as I saw them," Truly said. "When you called and asked me, that was the first time I—"

"But if you didn't post it, how could you . . . you know what? Whatever, it doesn't matter. It's no big deal," I told her. "Natasha will get over it."

"Her mom told mine that she's crying," Truly said. "She won't come out of her room."

Evangeline rolled her eyes. "What a drama queen."

"Maybe she's really upset," Lulu argued, bouncing around in place. "Should we call her?"

"And say what?" Evangeline asked.

"We could say, come on over," Truly suggested. "Maybe. If—I mean, it's fine with me, if you guys don't mind."

"How is that not incredibly awkward?" Evangeline asked.

Truly was chewing on her fingers, and flicking her eyes up to my face, as if I were in charge somehow over who could come to her house or not.

"Do whatever you want," I said. "We don't care. It's one afternoon. Whatever. Sure. So. Henry seems like a nice guy."

"Henry? Yeah, he is nice. Not everybody realizes that. It's . . . anyway. So you think I should call Natasha?"

"Maybe you should," Lulu said, leaning forward. "What does your mom think?"

"That I should call her."

"Okay, then," Lulu said. "You probably should."

Truly popped up and rushed in her tiny steps down the hall, I guess to get her phone or use the one in the kitchen or whatever. I took my phone out of my pocket and texted Clay: *Remind me to be partners with you next time. Too much Drama here.*

I put my phone away, and also my thoughts about what my sister would say about why I really wanted to be partners with Clay and what a hypocrite I am for thinking other people should own their feelings, while I refuse to, myself.

But I have a good reason: what I feel is irrelevant. So owning my feelings is pointless. I'm not confident like Hazel, flying my freak flag without caring what anybody else thinks, if they like me or don't, or like me but *not in that way.* Or people judging me about my family's failure. I try to believe I'm strong, brave, cool—but the fact I never really thought of until now is, I'm actually none of that. I'd rather play it safe than take a chance of Clay friendzoning me. It would get so awkward if he found out anything, and he'd be nice about it, sure, but something would be lost, between us. Ease.

It would be like having nine and a half fingers. Not fatal, not horrible, but something would always be off, missing, wrong.

TRULY

ONE NIGHT IN fifth grade when I was sleeping over, Natasha had fallen asleep but I was up reading in the trundle bed when her mom came to check on us. *I love you like my own,* she'd whispered, while she braided my hair so it wouldn't tangle while I slept. After she left, I thought for a sec that Natasha was awake, but when I looked again, her eyes were definitely closed and her breathing was slow, steady. I lay there for a long time with my heart pounding horribly. I'm not sure why I felt so bad, so caught.

Today when I called Natasha to ask her to come over and join us, she didn't answer her cell so I called the house phone. Her mom answered. She said no, I could not speak with Natasha. "It's important," I said.

"I saw what you posted," her mom hissed. "What is wrong with you?"

"I wanted to—"

"I don't really care what you want," she interrupted.

"I'm sorry," I managed.

She hung up on me.

I sat down on the kitchen floor and cried. Luckily Mom was upstairs dealing with Molly, who was having a tantrum about something, so she didn't know I was falling apart. I am the easy one in my family, the no-trouble kid, the one who is Mom's break, her sunshine. She calls me that, her little ray of sunshine, her butterfly. The last thing she needed is me having trouble, too.

When I heard Mom's feet on the stairs, I dashed to the bathroom to hide.

I obviously have to figure out what the heck happened with that thing I supposedly posted because I really didn't. Nobody believes me. So much that I have started to wonder myself. I definitely have no memory of it. Could I have posted two pictures and multiple comments without knowing?

If that's possible, how can I ever trust myself one bit? How can anyone trust me? And how can I trust anyone? If people can just do things they don't mean to do and then honestly have no memory of doing them, how can there not be complete chaos all the time?

Thoughts of chaos make me feel like puking.

On the bus ride home, Evangeline clearly didn't believe me. When I swore on my life I didn't post either of those things about who was coming over, she suggested maybe I sleep-posted it. That's a thing. She saw it on the news: people post stuff in their sleep. She might do an extra-credit science project on it. I said I'd be happy to work with her on it if she wants a partner because now I am really intrigued.

"Intrigued?" Evangeline asked.

I started to shrug but stopped myself, not wanting to look like I was copying Brooke and also not wanting to admit I had already edited that word when I said it. If *intrigued* is not an okay word, even to Evangeline, who watches the news apparently, how awkward was my original draft: *suppressing a panic attack at the possibility that I might be psychotic?*

So instead I forced my mouth into a smile and said, "Sure, I mean, what if I sleep-post more mean or embarrassing things?"

"That would suck," Evangeline agreed.

"I better hide my computer from myself when I go to bed, from now on," I said.

"Good idea," she agreed. I know she wasn't threatening me but she has a very serious face and huge muscles.

And now here I was, hiding not my computer from myself but instead myself from my guests, in my own downstairs bathroom. Not. Good. I looked at myself in the mirror. I did not look like "the awesome one in pigtails." I did not look like a wise goddess who could lead a hero through a city. I looked like a nine-year-old with a horrendous cold.

I filled up the sink with cold water and dunked my face in, holding my breath for as long as possible, thinking, I can handle this. Don't breathe. In a minute I will march myself back out there to these new friends who are sitting in my family room waiting for me to be a good host and come up with great ideas for our History Day project, which was the reason they even invited me to join their group to begin with. Good ideas on school projects. Do the work for the group. That's what I can do. It's not awesome but it's something. It's a little like being the kid who plays the dog in pretending games in elementary school. Not the doomed princess or the cruel stepmother, the wise spymaster or the evil wizard or the brave scout. The dog.

Like Henry. In elementary school, when he still had friends, he was always the dog. He wouldn't stop barking. Kids got annoyed. He crawled around on hands and knees and lifted his leg, pretending to pee in corners. My parents had to go in and talk with the school psychologist.

I used to be the princess or the sorcerer. Sometimes even the younger sister tragically dying of a disease in the Wild West or the Renaissance.

I stood up, gasping for breath, and grabbed the towel. Need to breathe overcomes willpower, again. Rubbing my face dry, I swallowed hard. I reminded myself to be good, light, fun. The dog is a decent part to play. At least it's a part. And I won't pretend to pee in the corner, at least. I don't think I will, anyway.

Who knows?

Oh, god. I can't. Can't deal. Can't hide that I am not at all cool, not light and fun and easy to be around. Can't keep up. Not even nice and loyal like a dog.

Pull yourself together, Truly, I whispered to myself in the mirror. *Pretend to be fine. Everything depends on that.*

JACK

IN FIFTH GRADE, I was a fat kid. I knew it, and not just because the kids in my class called me Jumbo. I pretended that didn't bother me.

When my best friend Russell explained to me why I didn't get invited to his birthday party, I pretended that didn't bother me either. He said he was only allowed to have a limited number of guests. That didn't make me feel any better, that I didn't make the cut, whatever it was. He was the only kid I'd invited to my birthday just the month before. But I was just like, oh, sure, no big deal.

My dad had taken off to go hang out on the beach in Florida a few months before my tenth birthday. He really liked bumming around on the beach, he said, and he didn't feel old enough to be a dad.

I started staying up until Mom went to bed, slipping out each half hour pretending to go to the bathroom. I was really just checking if she was going to bed yet or still sitting at the table staring into space or at a pile of bills. She took me to the doctor to see if there was something wrong, that I was going to the bathroom so much. There wasn't. But the doctor said I should make an effort to cut down on the processed food and empty calories, maybe get some more exercise. I promised I would, mostly so my mom would have one fewer thing to worry about. Anyway I told her that for my birthday party I wanted to invite just Russell over and we could make a birthday cake together, from scratch, no processed anything. I was just starting to get into cooking then, after the visit to the doctor's. Also I didn't want her to spend a bundle and deal with lots of kids coming over.

So Russell made my cut of one person. And I didn't make his cut of I didn't know how many. Which felt bad enough.

But then it turned out he'd invited all the boys in the fifth grade except me.

We moved away from there that June. Not because of Russell. My mom got a better job here and it's nearer to my grandparents and we really needed a fresh start. Over that summer, I started working out a lot, building up to a five-mile run (the distance to my grandparents' house) plus sit-ups, pull-ups, and push-ups. My jiggly belly was gone by September, and I was as tall as Mom, who wasn't staying up late crying anymore. I made travel soccer and hoops right away.

The kids here don't know I was a fat kid, the one kid whose best friend back in fifth grade didn't invite him to the birthday party everybody else got to go to, with paintball, which I probably would have loved.

Nobody calls me Jumbo here. They just say Jack, and to all of them here I'm a nice guy, good at sports, and the undisputed lunch-making champion. I guess I'd say I'm in the popular group, but there's not a sharp division here of popular versus unpopular kids like in my old school. There are the sporty guys and the theater/music guys, with lots of overlap, and then the keep-to-themselves guys. But all the boys get along. Like if we're on a project together for History Day, we get into groups and make our posters. Everybody's included. Somebody says something at lunch? We're like a collection of bobble-heads, all nodding, yeah, true, good point. And then if somebody says, well yeah, but, the opposite of that, we all do the bobble-head thing again, yeah, true, that's a decent point, too.

At least that's how it feels to me. I'm always on the lookout for somebody being left out but I could be missing something. It's possible there are boys here I don't know that well who feel like the odd man out.

The girls have more of that kind of thing going on.

I can't tell if Truly Gonzales is starting to like me yet. I'm doing my best to act friendly and relaxed around her. Mom suggested that behavior instead of bringing Truly a little present of any kind. I busted her knee wide open and she needed two kinds of stitches for that, but still Mom thought an apology was sufficient and a gift could backfire in my goal of making Truly think positively about me.

So I am just going to hang on to this bracelet I bought for $16.99.

It's a very delicate chain that I think would look really pretty on Truly's tiny wrist. But I will just wait and see how things go in our friendship, as Mom suggested. Mom is very smart about relationships.

In the jewelry store where I secretly went to buy a gift for Truly before Mom said not to, the lady behind the counter looked at me like I might knock stuff down or steal it. I was thinking that people shouldn't judge a book by its cover but I didn't make my game face at her. I smiled what my mom calls my charming politician smile instead and pointed at the most delicate little chain in the display case. "May I see that one, please?" I asked her.

Her lemon-butt mouth tightened, but she reached into the case and lifted out the bracelet I was pointing at. I opened my palm like a beggar. She placed the bracelet in the center of it, which was slightly dirty from recess.

I wasn't sure what you are supposed to do, to decide whether or not you want to buy a bracelet. I watched it for a thirty-count. It stayed still. So did I.

"Thank you, I would like this one please," I said. "To buy it, thank you."

She lifted the chain out of my palm, but even after it was gone I could still feel it there, cool and light as mist. Then I put my hand down by my side so she wouldn't think I was begging for spare change or a banana or something.

The lady started to put the bracelet in a small white paper

bag but stopped and turned just her head around to me, like an owl. "Is this for a special friend?" she asked.

I looked down at the counter and said, "Yes. It is." I thought she might say something jokey like, *Well good because it would not fit you,* or maybe mocking, like, *Oooo, you have a girlfriend!* So I was taking a deep breath and preparing to say that yes I am aware it wouldn't fit me or no I did not have a girlfriend.

But the lady didn't say anything. When I looked up again, she was sliding the small chain into a white box padded up with a cloud of cotton.

"How much extra is that?" I asked. I had twenty dollars left from what my grandfather gave me over the summer for all the yard work I helped him with, even though I said he absolutely did not have to pay me, but I wasn't sure how to calculate tax on the bracelet, and also I didn't want to spend every last bit. Sometimes I like to treat myself to a pack of sour power straws.

"It's free," the lady said. "My pleasure. I'm sure your friend will love the bracelet."

"I hope so," I said as she tied two ribbons around the box, a blue one and a silver, interlaced, and formed them into a loopy bow. "Thank you," I said.

"You're very welcome," the lady said as I was leaving with the box in a tiny white bag that dangled like a Christmas ornament from my fingers. "Be careful out there."

I wasn't sure if she was saying be careful of life in general or specifically that giving presents like delicate bracelets to girls might put a guy at risk of having his heart broken. So I just said, "Okay," and let the door close behind me.

I didn't show the box to my mom that night. During dinner, I just brought up the idea of maybe getting a small gift for Truly. The little box was bulging low in my sweatshirt jacket pocket, hidden. I was thinking I'd surprise Mom with it. Like a test run.

Mom was pretty clear, though, that it wasn't a great idea.

So I didn't show her. I slipped the box into my sock drawer after dessert, which was a molten chocolate chip cookie cake I had worked on all afternoon after I got home from the store. Soccer practice had been canceled because of rain, which is why I had time to go there, and also make the cake. Mom loved the cake. It was really delicious, even though we didn't have a double boiler for the chocolate and it was my first attempt at something with a molten center, which you really should have a double boiler for.

Now the box lives at the bottom back of my sock drawer and I feel a little like a traitor or a pirate, not telling Mom about it. I don't keep many secrets from her and this one feels big. It's like I'm betraying her or something. Like she might find it when she's putting away my clean socks for me, which I have told her she doesn't have to do anymore, I can do it—and she'll take that small white box with its ribbons out, and place it right in the center of the kitchen table. And I will see it sitting there when I get home and she won't even yell at me, she'll cry.

That's silly, I know. Why would Mom cry about that?

It's a nightmare I keep having, even when I'm not sleeping. Like when I used to dream about my dad coming back just to tell me he really left not because he loves the beach, or because of his age, but because I was a disappointment as a son. I'd run after him, trying to explain that I was just a little kid before he left! Little kids don't realize how annoying they're being. I would be way better as a son now! But I was shouting all those sorry excuses at his big broad back as he walked away, again and again. Or the other nightmare where Russell and everybody were standing on one side of the playground and they all pointed at me and laughed. Luckily I haven't had either of those lousy dreams in a long time.

But today on the playground, I thought of that old playground dream. We were playing catch instead of Salugi because unfortunately the teachers were out there enjoying the weather after the rain of the past few days. I was looking around after Mike missed an easy throw, and I saw that unbalance thing: most of us were on one side of the playground all together and Truly was sitting on the steps by herself, with her bum leg out to the side.

Mike lobbed me the ball after he got it from the bushes. I tossed it deep to Clay, who caught it easy, but before he could decide whether to throw it back to me or over to someone else I ducked my head and took a slow jog over toward where Truly was sitting on the steps.

I was wishing even though Mom thought it wasn't a great idea that I had that small white box in my sweatshirt jacket pocket again and I could give it to Truly and it would make her smile. She'd look a little confused, maybe, but then she would hold the box in her hands where it would look like a nice-size box, not a tiny thing like in my big paw. And she would open the ribbons slowly, untying them with expert delicate fingers, like a safecracker or a surgeon. And she'd be all flustered when she saw the bracelet and be all like, "Wow, Jack—thank you so much!" and maybe give me a hug or something for it. And then she'd put it on and wear it all the time from then on.

And I would always notice it there on her wrist.

But all I had in any of my pockets was a dollar seventy and my school ID. And probably some lint. Still, being the one kid not invited to Russell's party left a mark on me in the way that I don't like to see a kid sitting all alone. That's true even if it's not a person as smart and pretty and interesting as Truly Gonzales.

I sat down next to Truly. Because I didn't have the gift with me to hand over, I had to think of something to say to her instead, which I probably should have been working on during my jog across the playground instead of hashing over old experiences from when I was ten and lived in Ohio instead of here.

"Hi, Jack," Truly said, after I was sitting there beside her for a while, clasping and unclasping my fingers, resting my forearms on my quads and trying to think of a good thing to say.

"Hi, Truly."

My mom is probably right though. A gift at that point would have been awkward.

"How's your busted knee?" I asked her.

"Better," she said. "I get the stitches out today."

"That's good," I said.

"Really?" she asked.

"Well, that means it's healing, right?"

"I never had stitches before. I'm kind of scared of getting them removed. Did you ever have stitches?"

"Yeah." I showed her the scar on my forehead.

"Oh, no. What happened?" She was leaning close to my face to see the scar. It was the first time I ever felt proud of it, or happy I had it.

"I fell out of bed," I told her. "When I was four. I don't even remember it, but my mom says there was blood everywhere. I remember getting the stitches out, though."

"Was it awful?"

"No," I said. "My dad gave me a lollipop to suck on so I just focused on that and then it was done and I still got to keep sucking on the lollipop. I thought I'd have to give it back when they were done, but no."

Truly smiled at me. "They let you keep the half-eaten lollipop?"

"Yup. Pretty awesome, huh?"

"Didn't make you give it to the next kid who was getting stitches out?"

"Nope," I said. "No presucked lollipop for that kid. All for me."

"You're a lucky guy."

"True that."

She giggled a little, a throaty laugh.

"I wish I had a lollipop to give you," I said.

She blinked her eyes at me. A few times in a row, nice and slow. They have very long eyelashes.

"And I could keep it the whole time?" she asked.

"Uh, yeah," I said. Man, those eyelashes are seriously like Mr. Snuffleupagus on *Sesame Street*'s eyelashes. "All for you."

"I'll imagine it," Truly whispered. "The whole time they're yanking out the stitches, I'll close my eyes and imagine the—what flavor would it be, if you had a lollipop to give me?"

"Do you like watermelon?"

"My favorite."

"Mine, too," I said, looking down at my gripped fingers so I would stop staring at Truly's eyelashes. "I would give you a watermelon lollipop, if I could."

"Thanks, Jack," she said.

"You're welcome."

Then she didn't say anything else and I didn't want to ruin the perfection of that minute by accidentally saying well, it's funny you should mention a gift I might give you because I have one that I already bought and it is in my sock drawer right under a pile of tube socks. Don't worry; they're clean.

Toward the end of recess when my butt was really getting itchy from sitting so long on the brick steps, I stood up.

She got up, too, and said, "Well, see ya."

I am the second fastest kid in eighth grade, and Truly was limping. She is not fast even on her best day so I completely could have caught up with her. But I didn't try. I let her go. I watched her hobble toward the door and then push it open. Her narrow shoulders were slumped. I didn't know what was going on with her but obviously it was a lot, maybe more even than just worry about getting stitches out. And no imaginary lollipop from me seemed likely to lift that heaviness off her.

Maybe not even a very delicate and special bracelet could.

It's possible that I am a nicer person than I otherwise might have been because of some stuff I have gone through, as my mom says, and maybe everybody, even a person as sweet as Truly, has to go through some tough times in life. And bear them alone. My mom is really smart about stuff like life and hardships, so I am sure that is the truth. We have to appreciate our troubles, Mom says.

Maybe Truly just wanted to get away from me because she thinks I am a fat kid whose name should be Jumbo. I don't think so. I don't think that's it. I think she was just coping with some stuff privately and needed me to respect her solitude. I don't think she would think mean thoughts about me.

But how can I know? How can anybody ever really know

what another person is thinking inside his or her own skull?
I thought Russell was my best friend. I thought my dad was
going to snuggle me up and say *good night, sports fans* to me
every night until I was grown.

Obviously I had no idea.

NATASHA

"MAYBE TRY TO forget about it, Natasha," Lulu whispered to me. "Let it go."

"No, it's not that," I whispered back. Urgh. She can be so thick sometimes. But she was my best shot, the most gullible and agreeable, so I had to keep trying. We were at the back of the math room, trying to avoid the sub's occasionally lifted eyes. Mrs. Gerstein. Lulu kept her normally cartoon-expressive face unmoving, tilted down toward her desk.

"I just . . . " I tried sounding more sweet. "I wanted to warn you about Truly."

"Warn me?"

Yeah, warn you, you jerk. Could you give me a frigging break? "She's . . ."

Mrs. Gerstein looked up, so I bit my pencil and pretended to work on a stupid math problem until she sighed and went back to the novel she was reading.

"Truly felt terrible," Lulu whispered out the side of her puffy-lipped little mouth. "She did."

"She should! Not that I care," I whispered. "But come on, what kind of weasel posts a nasty thing like—"

"Maybe she was trying to be funny and it backfired," Lulu whispered.

"You don't know her like I do," I whispered back.

"Girls?" Mrs. Gerstein said. She's completely the best sub ever, because she gives exactly zero craps about what the students do, as long as we stay in our seats and don't bother her. Still, you want to keep it down so she doesn't feel obligated to take an interest in us.

"Sorry," I said, smiling at her. She nodded her fat head and went back to reading. We should make WE LOVE MRS. GERSTEIN T-shirts. That will be one of my projects if all goes according to plan and I fix the social mess in this stupid school. We could sell the T-shirts and raise money for an awesome middle-school graduation party, and everybody will be so into it. Or maybe for some charity. Everybody loves charity.

"Well, why did you want to bring her in, if she's such a terror?" Lulu asked me. "You're the one who said she was great, we'd love her."

I shook my head. Jack was sitting right in front of me, unmoving as a boulder. I couldn't tell if he was eavesdropping or not. He is clearly Team Truly, though, so I had to be careful. Luckily Brooke, Clay, Evangeline, and of course

Truly are in advanced math, so they couldn't butt in. Just us dummies, here. Still, I wanted to be focused and quick with Lulu. I had spent all night thinking this through but I still wasn't sure it would work.

"I wanted to give her a fresh chance," I whispered. "It's been a long time and, I figure, everybody deserves a second shot, right?"

Lulu is a big believer in doing the right thing. Also generosity. If anything would win her over, it would be this, I thought. Or else Plan B, which I wasn't launching until later.

Lulu nodded. "Sure."

I nodded, imitating Lulu's solemn nodding technique. Not to mock her, but just, it's kind of contagious. Also kind of funny. So serious. Please. Like she's a judge, passing judgment on me. Thank you, Your Honor.

"But I guess I was wrong." My voice was full of sorrow.

"Girls?" Mrs. Gerstein said again.

"Sorry," I said as sweet as I could. "We're trying to work through this problem together."

"Try independently, please," Mrs. Gerstein said.

"Sure," I answered. "Sorry, Mrs. Gerstein."

She picked up her novel again, though I am pretty sure her eyes were closed in front of it.

Lulu wrote in her notebook, which she tipped toward me. *What did she say when she called you yesterday?*

??? I wrote back, in my own notebook. *SHE NEVER CALLED.* All caps. I never write in all caps. All caps means yelling. But too bad.

166

The bell rang so we got up and gathered our books.

"She did," Lulu whispered. "After your mom called her mom. Truly was really upset and she said she felt terrible, and she wanted to call you and apologize. So she did."

I shook my head. "Nope. I had my phone with me the whole afternoon." That last part at least was true.

Lulu's unwaxed eyebrows approached each other on her forehead. She wasn't buying it. Damn, I was getting all muddled for no reason. Should always stay as close to the truth as possible to avoid exactly this. "Clay was texting with me," I said. "You can ask him if you don't believe me."

We got to the corridor and turned left in the Bedlam of between-classes. "Are you sure?" Lulu asked.

"Completely."

"She said she apologized."

"Never happened." Give me a break; she tried one damn time to call. Wow. Sainthood for her. Once and hanging up without leaving even a message is pretty frigging close to never calling. What if I didn't have her number programmed into my phone so I didn't know who was calling? Or maybe I was texting with somebody and didn't notice? It's practically the same as if she never made any effort at all.

"That's intense," Lulu whispered.

"I'm telling you," I said. "Totally intense. This is exactly what I'm saying."

"That's just nuts," Lulu said.

"It's my fault," I whispered, bending down toward Lulu's shiny-haired head.

"No," she said. "It's so not."

"I should have known better," I said. "And I hate to say this, but I honestly fear she's going to look for another victim, now that she succeeded in getting me kicked out of the Table."

"You really think she'd—"

"Or maybe she's not done hurting me yet. I don't know."

"Let me talk with Brooke," Lulu said.

"You don't have to," I said humbly. "I probably deserve it, though not for whatever reason Truly cooked up to poison Brooke against me. But just, like, for inflicting her on you all. I only hope she's still not done with me, and not turning her sights on you, or—"

Lulu put her heavy hand on my arm. "This isn't right," she said. "I'm gonna be late for Spanish but—don't worry. Okay? I got this."

"You're the best," I called after her. I was running late, too, obviously, but I took an extra few seconds to watch Lulu dash away, all full of righteous mission, with no idea what was ahead.

Because Plan B was only a few hours away.

HAZEL

AFTER MY PARENTS (holding hands; weird) and I got home from visiting my recovering grandmother in the hospital, where she is alive, conscious, and full of complaints about the incompetence of nurses she wants fired immediately, I checked all the sites and accounts I've been logging into. And there it was. The kind of thing I'd been expecting, waiting for, thinking if nobody got to it soon, I'd have to do it. Sometimes it feels like I have to do everything.

Do I have to be *everybody*?

Not this time! Such a relief. Somebody took a bit of initiative, finally. And I had to admit, it was a good one. I was impressed. I wouldn't have guessed Natasha was up to it, but maybe I'd been underestimating her.

It was Natasha's page on tellmethetruth.com. She had asked: *Does everybody hate me?*

She'd posted it just half an hour before I logged in. Five

minutes after she posted that pathetic question, somebody posted, anonymously of course: *Yes*

And then somebody else (or maybe the same person, pretending to be somebody else) added, one minute later, under it: *Everybody hates you! You have no friends AT ALL.*

And then, somebody else (or was it the same one person; impossible to know for sure but one could guess) added two minutes after that: *Loser*

I didn't write anything. But I left the window open. Watching. Waiting. I had a feeling I knew who posted each of those things.

I had a feeling they were all posted by the same person, in fact.

A tricky move. High risk, but smart. Respect on that one, respect where respect was clearly due. Because I felt pretty strongly that person, the person who posted all three horrible, mean, bullying answers was the same person who posted the question:

Natasha.

It was kind of brilliant, I thought, in its demented horribleness. She set herself up and then punched herself, virtually, in the face. In public.

If I was right, and I knew I was right, Natasha was waiting in front of a screen across town. Waiting in her room, a room I'd never seen but could imagine was probably cluttered and had a mirror or three, maybe recently redecorated in beige in an attempt at sophistication that failed because of the collages made with her (ex)-friends and the mess of clothes she probably had scattered across her floor. So undisciplined. I sat staring at my laptop's screen in my uncluttered pink mother-decorated-when-I-was-in-elementary-school-and-couldn't-object room. Natasha, I was certain, was across town in basically the same position as me—staring at the same screen, looking at her question and the three hideous responses to it.

Waiting.

Waiting for other people, people other than herself (and me; of course she didn't know I was logged on, or that I existed, particularly) to notice the post she'd put up, and the horrid responses she'd also put up, and spring into action.

How long could it take? In cyberspace, of course, each minute feels like forever. Refresh, refresh, *somebody respond! Come on!*

It took a full hour.

Finally, a response popped up, signed, from Lulu. Nice girl, Lulu. Not particularly interesting or creative, not an artistic type, but you never know. She's endured hardships and might have an ethical core. So I wasn't surprised to see her post first.

This is cyberbullying and whoever posted this: you know it can be traced rite? (Her misspelling, not mine.)

No response from Natasha or, well, Natasha. Other-Natasha. Bullying, imaginary-friend Natasha. I stopped pretending to do my homework and cupped my chin in my hands, to watch. A few seconds later, solid good Lulu added: *Natasha—everybody loves you. Don't listen to this troll.*

I waited some more, listening to my parents down the hall chatting together for the first time in a while. I wasn't sure what to make of *that*, but I was pretty sure the texting and screen capture and other connecty circuits were burning up between Lulu's house and the other Popular Table kids. It felt like watching popcorn in an uncovered pot, waiting for the little kernels to start exploding.

And, go.

BROOKE

MY PHONE WAS having seizures in my lap.

We're not allowed to have phones at the table. Mine was on silent, of course, but it was buzzing pretty much nonstop, and Mom had already looked over at me with one eye closed a couple of times. That woman has the best hearing of any living adult, I swear.

I asked to be excused and cleared my plate. At the sink I checked my phone. The whole screen was filled with texts. I went straight to the bathroom and locked the door.

All my psycho friends were freaking out. Those stupid apps. I swear I don't know why everybody likes them so much, but I had to sign in to see what everybody was losing their poops over.

It was Natasha's page on tellmethetruth.com. She had asked: *Does everybody hate me?*

What a stupid question, just fishing for reassurance. Why

does she have to be such a bait-breath? But then some genius had to answer, anonymously: *Yes*

Good one, Anonymous. Some of your poems are actually decent but that *Yes* was pure brilliance.

And then somebody else added, under it: *Everybody hates you! You have no friends AT ALL.*

And then, somebody else added: *Loser*

What is wrong with people? This is why we can't have nice things.

Of course by the time I logged in, everybody was posting under that crap stuff like *Don't be ridiculous* and *We all love you Natasha* and *Whoever wrote this is the loser* and so on. Like twenty of those. And then over on every other site, of course, everybody was rallying around Natasha. Because, yeah. I added my bit: *Haters gonna hate,* and then, in case that could be taken the wrong way: *We love you Natasha! Ignore this useless zero.*

Lulu had texted me about twenty times in the past half hour, begging me to call her. She picked up on the first ring.

"Hey," I whispered, turning the sink on full blast to muffle the sound. My dad is not a big fan of kids disappearing from the table, especially when grandparents are over, possibly to lend some money to tide us over. And double-especially to use phones.

"Here's the thing," Lulu said. "Natasha kind of predicted this. Today. She thinks it's Truly who wrote that crap about her."

"Truly?" I asked. "No way."

"I don't know," Lulu said. "She posted about us all going

over there, and then denied it."

"Yeah," I had to admit. "But didn't Truly post something nice? I saw . . ."

"Yeah," Lulu said. "Natasha predicted she would do that, too."

"But does that prove . . ."

"We're gonna meet tomorrow at the wall, early, okay?"

"Yeah," I said. "Thanks, Lulu," I added, and hung up.

I turned off the water but sat against the door, trying to think this through, whether I had been completely wrong about Truly being just kind of a nice, smart, slightly wonk-ish, maybe boring person. And Natasha being awful. Maybe Natasha hadn't even written that nasty e-mail to Truly, diss-ing her brother and sister. Holy crap. Hadn't thought of that before. What if Truly wrote it herself and forwarded it to me?

No. Why would she do that?

Urgh, I hate everybody.

Why can't people just be normal to one another? And predictable? And say what they think? Unless it's mean or hopeless, in which case, get over it.

I stared at my phone. Then I took a selfie, making the face I felt like—eyes crossed, tongue out. I sent it to Clay. Then I randomly sent it to Hazel, too.

I just felt like it. I don't know why. Maybe because Hazel is probably the only kid I know who's not involved at all in the whole online mess.

CLAY

THEY GOT AN e-mail from the school about algebra. Nobody in my family has ever before today gotten a progress report. They send them if your child is at risk of failing a class. Mom was a bit stuck on the discovery that they send an e-mail notice. "I never knew they did that!" she mentioned. More than once.

"They sure are something," I said, after the third time.

Dad was less delighted with the diligence of the school. Also, of me.

"You can't glide through life forever on your ample charm, Clay, flirting with teachers and getting away with lazy lack of effort," Dad started. Then he kept going. Words, words, words. They'll get me a tutor if I need it. But I have to pull my weight. I hid my problems from them, which is dishonest. Blah blah blah. I sat there in the kitchen with my hoodie hood up. Bucketfuls of words barfed from his mouth about what a piece of crap I am, worthless, shameful. Not those exact words, of course, but obviously that's what they meant, under all their concern-trolling. I'm paying attention to all the wrong stuff. Not paying attention to the important things, like algebra, and whatever else Dad was listing.

Progress report. What a stupid name for it.

Mom joined in. She was blaming herself for not being more on my case or some such nonsense, so condescending. Obviously she was mad at me, but she was saying she wasn't—she was mad at herself and worried about me. Please. I stopped listening.

I watched their eyes flickering to each other's. Them against me.

They're a team, with JT as their quarterback and mascot. Me? I'm the *problem*.

When they ran out of words, Dad sent me to my room. Okay by me. I could work twenty-five hours a day and I'd still never be as smart and successful as them, or my brother. What's the use? Why even try?

On my way up the stairs, my phone buzzed. Brooke with her eyes crossed like such a goof. Yay, Brooke. Leaning against my closed door inside my room, I sent back a picture of myself with x's drawn over my eyes and a big blue frown over my mouth.

Brooke called me two seconds later. "What happened?"

So I told her. The whole story. And, okay, I fully expected her to feel bad for me or just say stuff to make me laugh and forget. But she was like, "So why don't you just do your damn homework?"

"Thanks, pal," I said. "Whose side are you on?"

"Seriously," she said.

I flopped down on my bed. "What? Who put the bug up your . . ."

"It's just, you're making a problem for yourself when . . ."

"When what?"

"Nothing." Then she shouted, "*Leave me alone!*"

"You called me!"

"No, Margot's frigging pounding on the—*I'm in here!*"

"Are you on the toilet?" I started laughing. "You're calling me while pooping? That is hilarious."

"No! I, it's the only place I can get any priva—*fine!* Hold on, Clay, I'm not done with you I'm going to the basement hold on hold on."

"Did you at least wash your hands?"

"Shut up," she said. "I wasn't—ugh. Did you see all the crap online about Natasha?"

"No," I said. "I was too busy getting my ears chewed off by my parents. What happened?"

"Bunch of drama. The Internet is gonna break. People being stupid."

"Same ole stuff?"

"And then some." Brooke said. "I'm just—Here's the thing, okay? I am down in the disgusting basement and I have no shoes on and everybody's freaking out online so I only have a sec. So listen quick. Okay?"

"Okay."

"You know the problem with you?"

"Too charming?" I asked.

"Hardly. It's JT."

"My brother is what's wrong with me?"

"Your *idea* of him. You're so busy protecting yourself from falling short of how awesome JT is, you won't even do your frigging homework! You're good at math. Maybe do a bunch of practice problems each night. Just work at it, you know? Take some responsibility."

"What if I can't get it through my thick head no matter what?"

"Maybe you just have to keep trying."

"I'm better at hanging out than slogging away at stuff."

"Maybe you've just had more practice at hanging out."

"Definitely. My only skill."

"You're smart, Clay. You're just scared. You think your brother is like the Second Coming, but he's just a guy. Why are you so in love with him?"

"What?" I couldn't believe my ears. "I am so not! In love with JT? Are you tripping? Are there weird fumes down in your basement? Evacuate, dude!"

"I'm completely serious, for once."

"In love with—my brother? Ew, I don't even miss him. I'm glad he's away, kind of. I'm just pissed because now the pressure's all on me."

My mom was knocking on my door. "Clay?"

"Sorry, Mom."

"I think you should be doing your homework," Mom said.

"Yeah, I know!" I yelled. "Brooke is giving me the same lecture."

"Good," Mom said. "I'm making popcorn, when you're ready."

"My mom's making me guilt popcorn," I whispered to Brooke.

"Well," she said. "Sucks to be you."

"Yeah," I agreed. "It kind of does."

"You really don't miss him?"

"I do." I closed my eyes. "I miss him. Whatever."

"I know you do."

"But not . . ."

"Not what?" she asked. Her voice was soft.

"Sometimes? Not as much as I thought I would."

"Yeah," she said.

I waited for her to try to convince me that was good, or that it is what it is, or not to be such a drama queen about it, or that I was a selfish jerk who didn't really love my brother if I didn't miss him as terribly as I'd thought I would, sometimes. But she didn't say anything.

"Do you think it means I'm, like, a crappy brother?" I whispered.

"No," she said.

"Or that we're not as close as I thought?"

"Maybe it just means you're dealing," she said.

"Yeah." I said. "Maybe. He's right, of course. My father. About me."

"That you should do your homework?" Brooke asked. "Yeah, he's a certified genius, that one. What an insight. I never could've come up with—"

"No, that, you know, I'm lazy. That I just do what's easy."

"Easy stuff is easier," she said.

"He's right about absolutely everything, as always, like you," I said.

"Ha," she said. "As if."

"Except for one thing."

"What's that?"

"That I don't care. That I don't mind possibly failing eighth grade math. That it doesn't bother me that I'm the stupid one in a family where the only thing that matters is how smart you are."

"Clay . . ."

"If he really thinks that? Maybe I'm not the only idiot in the family after all," I said, and then, "I gotta go. Sorry."

I hung up and was about to turn off my phone when it rang in my hand. It was JT. He wanted to FaceTime.

Just what I wasn't up for. "Nice timing, dude," I said instead of hello.

"I miss you, too," he said.

We just hung out on the phone, talking about nothing, for a while. It was good to see his face, in spite of everything. And to make him laugh.

It was kind of like if you get one of those rocky tables and every time you put your elbows on it, the drinks all spill, but then somebody has the good sense to fold up a napkin and shove it under one of the legs and then everything's fine.

NATASHA

I KNEW THEY'D rally to my side if somebody went this far in being mean to me. And really, all I was doing was putting it in text, on the screen, out in cyberland for everybody to see exactly how they were making me feel.

It wasn't a lie so much as a, like, boom. There it is. This is basically what you're saying or how you're all acting: like you hate me, I'm a loser, I should die. That's exactly how it felt when I was kicked out of the group, just dumped and unfriended, left like roadkill to slump off and die in the library by myself.

So: how do you feel seeing it right out there?

Bad. They felt bad. I knew they would. They're not heartless. And I think they do still care about me. Maybe Evangeline doesn't. Maybe she's the real one behind the kicking me to the curb. She doesn't care about me. But she's tough, and Brooke knows her, loves her, more than Truly. Truly was the one I could turn them against, not Evangeline, so I could get back to where I belonged.

And Truly deserved it anyway.

So when my mother came bursting into my room holding her own laptop demanding to know what was happening on my pages online, I didn't tell her that I had posted the insults. Because then who knows. Maybe she would drag me back to therapy or tell me I was a sick duck or get all disgusted with me even more than if she thought a friend did it.

"Did Truly post these mean things about you now?"

"That's what people seem to think," I said.

"That little . . . what is going on with her lately?"

"I don't know."

"Well, I don't *care*," Mom said. "You reached out to her and invited her to join in with *your friends* . . ."

"Yup," I said. "That'll teach me to be generous, huh?"

"It wasn't enough she had to make a complete fool of you, with that obnoxious *you're invited whoops no you're not* nonsense? Now she's posting just flat-out nastiness?"

I nodded.

Mom slammed her laptop down on my desk and groaned. Fully on my side. Ready to fight. For me.

"And now, did you see this? She just posted a whole bunch of *oh, Natasha we love you* baloney."

"She did?" I sat up. "Where?"

"*We*, she said. *We love you Natasha.* Look!"

I looked at Mom's computer. She was open to a site where

Truly had posted a very cute photo of all of us, with her cheek right next to mine. We both looked pretty. "Huh."

"Who does she thinks she's talking for?" Mom was saying while I enlarged the photo. "We? We? *We* love you. Like she's suddenly, what? Homecoming queen? Spokesmodel of the clique *you* invited her into? Where does this girl get her nerve? Just like her mother, she's turning everybody against us."

I clicked onto another site. Truly's photo was there, too, and also one of the two of us in second grade, holding hands and kissing each other on the lips.

Mom rolled her eyes. "Give me a freaking break."

"Right?" I said. The likes were clicking up fast. "Though we did look cute, don't we? Awww, look at us."

"Nobody's buying her bull, I hope," Mom said. "Especially you."

"No way," I said.

"She's bullying you, Natasha. But what she's forgetting is that hurt people hurt people."

I nodded.

"We have to hit her back. I don't know how. But we can't let her get away with this."

Great minds. "I was thinking, actually, that we could post, anonymously, somehow, that we know she's the one who posted that mean stuff about me."

"Hmmm," Mom said. "Yes. Smart. I like it."

"Really?" I asked. "And maybe also start some rumors . . . ?"

"How do we do it?"

I intertwined my arms with hers and typed the words I'd been planning.

Mom giggled. "Nice," she said, and hit enter.

As we waited for the reaction, she braided my hair for the first time in forever. Like she did to Truly's hair one night in fifth grade when they thought I was asleep. I closed my eyes and wished I had Rapunzel hair so it would take her all night. But we had more work to do, anyway.

TRULY

I FELL ASLEEP in front of my computer last night and dreamed that everybody was joking around at the lunch table but I couldn't make any sense of their words. Every time I tried to say anything, even *yeah*, the conversation screeched to a halt and they all stared at me. I knelt down to pretend to tie my shoe so they'd look away. When I stood up, they were gone.

I was alone.

My bag was gone, too, with my phone, my money, my school ID all in it. I had nothing. I wasn't in the cafeteria anymore, then. I don't know where I was.

I felt lost and scared, but also ashamed. They had ditched me on purpose, I realized, and it felt like they were completely justified. Like I had done something similar to somebody.

Hazel.

I had been denying it to myself, all this time, the awfulness of what I'd done. Hazel was odd, I'd been assuring myself. Hazel is awkward and overly dramatic. So how I treated her is pretty much her own fault.

But the truth is I just basically dumped her for a better offer.

For all my acting nice, blameless, yes, as Natasha accused: innocent—I deep down inside had this secret haughty attitude like, well, if you worked your butt off like I do, Hazel, maybe you'd have better grades, and if you tried harder to think about other people's interests and feelings maybe you'd get to sit at the Popular Table too. *I deserve the success I have in this life*, I reminded myself constantly. I studied hard not just the school stuff but the social stuff as well.

I had watched and read and researched and spent a lot of time thinking about how to be cool, how to fit in. Maybe Hazel didn't think that's important or maybe she just couldn't manage to achieve it. And, in the dream, I wasn't thinking, *Oh, how awful; I should be more patient and kind.* I was thinking, *Well, tough.* Hazel always talks about the amazing things she'll achieve, but maybe someday I'll be the one who's famous, not her. I'll write a book about friendship politics where the popular kids aren't libeled as bullies and the weird annoying kids aren't hailed as saints.

Maybe the popular kids are popular because they're nice and fun. So people want to be around them. Did you ever think of that, Hazel? Yeah. Sucks to suck. And it's good to be chosen. So, ha on you and hooray for me.

And then *wham* it got dark and cold, and I realized oh, wait, I am not the strong, right, popular winner anymore.

I'm the one who was abandoned. The one the Populars didn't want to be around. Some clowns started chasing me. They were laughing and pointing.

I ran hard, trying to get away. A herd of llamas watched me run past, staring with their huge cold eyes. "It was all a joke," one of the llamas told me. And I knew it was true, even though it was a llama saying so: it was all a joke.

Those popular kids were never my friends. It was an experiment, a cruel trick. One of them had said to the rest, Hey, do you think we could take some Random and make her think she's in with us? They picked me, and I fell for it.

Everybody knew. They never even liked me. Everybody was laughing at my obvious obliviousness the whole time.

Even the llamas.

Or maybe, I thought, in the dark noisiness of this freaky rodeo/carnival dream place, it was worse than that. I was in some kind of moral experiment, being tested for what kind of person I was. MORAL HAZARD, the sign above a carnival booth said, in bright flashing lights. It was a throw-darts-at-balloons booth called MORAL HAZARD. It was a test to see how I handled being wanted by people who had shunned me before.

A guy with very few teeth handed me a fistful of darts. I didn't want to but I had to throw them. The first few darts didn't even reach the wall of balloons. I had no chance of getting the big stuffed dog or the blow-up alien. What's the point? Toothless guy wouldn't let me quit. *Throw and miss*, he said. He opened his horrible mouth wide and laughed at me. *Just like you missed every nuance, every inside joke,* Toothless mocked. The next dart I threw hit Toothless in his chest. He started bleeding, gushing blood from his chest—but he kept laughing at me.

I dropped the final dart and started running, searching for an exit or a familiar face, but the lights started swirling and the music got all weird and disharmonic. I was crying and tripping over stuff, bumping into people, but I kept running until I heard my name.

It was coming over the loudspeaker. I stopped. Everybody stopped and listened. I was hoping it was my mom, that she still loved me and was looking for me and would save me, help me find a way out. But no.

The voice, unrecognizable, thundered: *Gabriela Gonzales! You don't deserve to be called Truly anymore, do you? How do you like it when you are the one who can't keep up? Gets dumped? Where's your righteous indignation and social Darwinist cool now, Butterfly?*

What? What does that even mean?

That's when I woke up in a cold sweat, terrified. I had slept through my alarm.

Just a dream, I told myself, rushing to get ready for school. But even the quick hot shower and rough apricot scrub Mom had bought me special couldn't clean the clammy sweat and dream residue off me. I had to go to school still reeking of it.

BROOKE

"NATASHA'S MOM IS tracing the anonymous responses," Lulu whispered.

"She can do that?" Evangeline asked.

Lulu nodded, leaning in closer. "Natasha was texting me until like two A.M. Her mom is ninety-nine percent sure it was Truly who posted all those mean things to Natasha."

"Seriously?" Evangeline asked. "Yikes." She blew out a mouthful of breath.

"I know it, right? Pretty sick," Lulu said.

"If it's true," I said.

"Ninety-nine percent is pretty tight," Lulu said. "And she's obviously not the only person who thinks so. Did you see the things people were posting about Truly?"

"Yeah," Evangeline and I both said.

Truly had posted a bunch of stuff like: *Natasha, don't*

listen to this nonsense—you are a good, kind, loving person and who-ever wrote this is the loser not you!

Same as we'd all done.

But under some of Truly's comments, some people we didn't know (probably with fake accounts, I was guessing) wrote: *Nice try Truly* and then: *Yeah, Truly. Nobody's buying your innocent act anymore.*

Evangeline nodded. "I saw that stuff. That was harsh. Do you think Natasha wrote that?"

Lulu shook her head. "I was texting with her when it was posted. I told her about it and she didn't believe me at first. I had to tell her where to look."

"So who posted it?" Evangeline asked. "Those were obviously fake names, plus a lot of anonymous posts."

"Maybe somebody who knows that Truly really did post those nasty things about Natasha?" Lulu suggested.

I shrugged. "Like who?"

"Maybe Jack," Lulu said.

"No way," I said. "He loves her!"

"Maybe he did," Lulu said. "But she's supposedly been texting with Clay," Lulu whispered. "A lot."

"Really?' I asked.

"Natasha said Truly's been bragging about it."

We all looked over to where Truly had been sitting alone. She wasn't alone anymore. She and Clay were sitting together, completely flirting.

Evangeline and Lulu both tipped their heads at me,

squinching up their mouths in sympathy.

"I don't care!" I said.

"Truly knows you guys like each other," Evangeline whispered gravely.

Lulu nodded. "She told me she thought you're such a cute couple."

"Same," whispered Evangeline.

"You guys were talking about me?"

"She brought it up," Lulu said.

"To me, too," Evangeline said. "And now she's after him? After using Jack? Not cool on so many levels."

We all turned to see Clay leaning closer to Truly, whispering.

"Come on, let's go in," Evangeline said. "Everybody sucks."

"Except us," Lulu said.

"Yeah," I said. "Because we're so awesome."

"Aren't we?" Evangeline asked.

"Slut," Lulu whispered toward Truly as we passed her flirting with Clay, who is fully just a friend and never will be anything more to me ever.

CLAY

WHEN I GOT to school this morning, all the girls were in a tight huddle, whispering. Including Brooke, who I really wanted to talk to about last night, about what she had said about I should just do my homework and what I did, after, because of it. But she was clearly dealing with some Lulu crisis so I went by. Catch her later, I figured.

Truly Gonzales was sitting by herself off to the side, chewing on her fingers. Huh. Jack and Dave and those guys weren't around, so I went and sat down next to Truly. "I used to bite my nails," I said.

"Me, too," she said. I smiled. She pulled her fingers away from her mouth.

"You okay?" I asked her.

"Sure."

"What's wrong?"

She started to shrug but stopped. We sat there not talking for a while. I didn't really know her that well and never actually had a conversation with her before so I wasn't sure what to talk about. I'm the last one to make somebody talk if she doesn't want to, so I figured we'd just sit there until the bell rang. I looked for Jack to say sorry I'd forgotten again to do the History Day thing, but he was nowhere.

The girl clump started walking. I looked up, thinking I'd catch Brooke's attention, maybe walk in with her. But her eyes were straight ahead. She didn't even notice me.

As they passed, Lulu muttered *slut* at me.

Great.

Natasha must've fed them more crap about what a terrible person I am. Funny my dad thinks my problem is that I am *too* charming. #thestruggle. Please. But still I wasn't sure why Brooke would be ignoring me.

I guess Truly heard what Lulu called me because she whispered, "Someone once said, if you want a friend, get a dog."

"That's a good one," I said. "At least I have my dog."

"Harry Truman," she said.

"Huh?" I was like, does she think my dog's name is Harry Truman?

"Harry Truman," she repeated. "I was . . . I know who said it, actually. Harry S. Truman. I'm a nerd. Now you know."

"Okay."

"He actually said, 'If you want a friend *in Washington,* get a dog.'"

"Oh," I said.

"Natasha says nobody likes a know-it-all so I've been try-ing to . . ."

"Be a know-nothing?"

"I guess."

"Seems kinda . . . dumb, actually," I said, to myself as much as to her. "As a goal. Seem stupider than you are. Even if you achieve your goal, you suck."

"Yeah." She shook her head, which made her ponytail sway. "Whatever, anyway, obviously that doesn't work either, so I may as well own up. Harry S. Truman. Go ahead and hate me I don't even care anymore."

"I thought you were doing Benedict Arnold."

"What?"

"For the, for History Day."

"I am. We are. I was. I don't know."

"Okay," I said.

"I like Harry Truman."

"Nice."

"What? You're, what, a big, Roosevelt fan? Or Dewey?"

"Who?"

"Nothing. I just, I don't know . . ." She took a deep breath. "I was just thinking about, you know, friends. I'm sorry. I had a bad dream last night."

"Oh," I said.

"Is why I'm in a weird mood."

I didn't want to say, Yeah, and also your friends were in

a tight huddle and they kept looking over here at you, all suspicious. And now they walked into school without you. So instead I said, "We might be doing Harry S. Truman."

"Really?"

"Yeah," I said. "Him and his dog. And, maybe, his favorite foods. Jack might cook them. If—What were his favorite foods?"

"You're making this up right now, right?" she asked.

"I have until fifth period," I protested. "You're pretty good at math, right?"

"I guess," she said. She sounded kind of disappointed in herself about it. "Of course. You?"

"Did you know that algebra means 'the reunion of broken parts'?"

"No," she said, a small smile tipping her lips up. "Does it really?"

"Yeah," I said. "From the Arabic words meaning 're-union' and 'broken parts.'"

"That's actually awesome," she said.

"Yeah. Well, that's all I got, algebra-wise. Maybe I'll put that down, see if I get some extra credit. I'll need it."

The bell rang. She stood up smiling. "'The reunion of broken parts,'" she said. "I really like that. Ha. I'm a mess of broken parts, feels like. Could use a reunion."

"Sorry," I said. "You what?"

"Nothing," she said. "Just, thanks. Maybe the answer's in the algebra textbook."

"There's an answer key at the back," I said. "And I did the homework for once, if you need the answers."

She laughed. "Yeah right, if only those were the answers I needed. Thanks, Clay."

"Sure," I said. "Any time."

JACK

"YOU LIKE HER?" I asked Clay. Point blank.

"Who?" he asked.

Who. Sure. "Truly."

Clay shrugged. He and Brooke, all they do is shrug.

"Man up, man," I said. "Yes or no."

"No," Clay said. "She's nice. Strange but nice. A little sad, maybe, probably because of all the . . ."

"I like her," I said.

"Okay," he said. "I don't. Not like . . . We were just talking. About algebra."

"I know what all the girls are saying she did, what they're saying she is. It's not true, none of it. Are you. . . ."

"Am I . . . what?" Clay asked.

"Plotting something." They're always plotting something. The girls and Clay along with them. Clay is like one of the girls, he's in so thick with them.

"Plotting?" Clay asked, like I was stupid, or kidding. He said *plotting* like it was *pooping*.

"Yeah," I said. "Plotting. What."

"Jack." He smiled, punched my arm lightly. "Come on. Chill."

I wasn't letting him smile me out of being pissed at him, though, the way he does to the girls and even a lot of the teachers. No way. I leaned toward him, with my feet planted far enough apart that nobody could knock me over if he tried. "You do whatever Brooke tells you to, so—"

"Hey," Clay interrupted.

"So I'm asking," I told him. "Are you planning something against Truly?"

"Like what?" he asked, lowering the front of his head and giving me that snarky smile. "Some kind of terrorist . . . situation?"

"I'm serious," I said, soft and slow. "She didn't do those things."

"What things?" he asked.

"Post mean stuff about Natasha. I know her. She wouldn't do that. On my honor."

"Okay," Clay said. "On your . . . Sure."

"Don't do anything to her," I warned him.

"I didn't," Clay said, looking down the hall toward smart kids' math class, where he needed to go. Where he had class with Truly. "I wouldn't," he told me. "Chill, Jack. Seriously. Okay? We cool?"

I stared at him hard for a few more seconds without answering, then turned around and went in, already late to dumb kids' math.

NATASHA

FAT LOT OF good all their sympathy does me if I'm still not invited to sit at their table at lunch. I didn't even look over there. I had a way better plan for lunch anyway: I was heading straight to Marilicia.

I know I'm the one who kicked her out last year, but come on, that was a long time ago. I think it's fair to say we all grew up a lot between seventh grade and eighth and, also, bygones.

If I joined up with Marilicia, we could start our own Popular Table. Maybe we could get Lulu to defect and come sit with us, and probably some of the guys. Maybe Dave Calderon, who I could totally flirt with and win over, probably. Maybe I could like him. Theo's too goofy, but maybe Mike Shimizu could sit with us if he could detach from Jack's heels. So what if Mike is short and serious? Some people probably like that. Why should he always have to be in Jack's shadow?

I could say that, maybe, flatter him. Maybe set him up with Marilicia. She's on the shorter, more serious side, too.

"Hey Marilicia," I said, catching her with one leg already over the bench.

"Hi, Natasha," she said, and sat down.

I stood there. I wasn't about to sit down at the freaks' table. I should have caught up faster so she wouldn't already be committed to it. But I wasn't giving up. Anyway, too late. I was there.

"How's it going?"

"Good," she said.

Her weird friends were checking me out. These kids were not going to be invited to our new Popular Table. Sorry. One of them had dark black hair, pale skin, red lips, liquid eyeliner. Another had a tight-shaved Afro and silver rings on both thumbs—I'm pretty sure those were both girls. A boy, right across from Marilicia, had his longish hair in loose dreads, and his orange button-down shirt rolled up at the sleeves past his elbows. A dark-eyed boy with a crew cut and deep blue T-shirt, smiled up at me in a welcoming way, at least. "Hi," he said.

"Hi," I answered, smiling at him. Cute. Still not invited.

"You gonna sit down?" he asked.

"I was just talking to Marilicia."

The dark-eyed boy nodded. "True."

I hunched down next to Marilicia, too tall, facing away from the table, and whispered, "I just, I really wanted to, belatedly, apologize."

Marilicia turned slowly and looked very intently at me but didn't say anything. No *that's okay* or *water under the bridge* or *we both did things we could share blame for* or anything. Just looked at me like she was looking in a mirror, checking for zits.

"For getting you, you know, kicked out of the Popular Table."

She smiled a tiny bit, so I figured I was on the right track.

"I think, I can't promise anything," I said. "But I think I could probably get you, you know, reinstated or whatever. Back in. Or, even better, well . . ." I smiled at her. Big smile, really friendly. She smiled back. "Maybe we could, you know, take a walk, talk about it," I suggested.

She laughed. A little chuckle at first, but it grew, slowly, until she was kind of honestly snorting and like almost coughing. Her freak friends all joined in, though a little less grossly, on Marilicia's laugh riot. All except for the black hair red lips girl, who just kept that doll-like blank expression on her face while slowly chewing whatever gross thing she was eating with chopsticks from her little plastic box. Seriously, chopsticks. The girl wasn't even Asian. At least not visibly Asian. So what point was she trying to make, chopsticks?

And what was she even wearing? It was like, weird. Made of scarves or something. Hello, nobody wears stuff like that.

"What?" I whispered. "What's so funny?"

Marilicia got a hold of herself. "It's just . . ."

She had to breathe a couple stray laughs out before she could explain her rude self. During that time I was realizing this plan completely sucked. Unfortunately, it was too late to escape.

"You come over here," Marilicia whispered to me. "You come like you're bringing me this, what? This, like, perfect fresh-picked strawberry. Or peach." Her hands made a bowl shape. "A peach you just picked off a tree, the most perfect peach anybody has ever picked, and you carry it lovingly, carefully, across the cafeteria, across the fields, across God's green earth to give it to me, just to me. Here's this perfect peach, Marilicia, you say, and I am giving it . . . to you."

"Okay," I said. This girl was certifiable. A peach? What the . . . ?

"But that's not a perfect peach, you self-important asshole," she said.

"What?" I crossed my arms. "I never said anything about a peach!"

"It was a metaphor," Crew Cut helpfully informed me.

"What's a metaphor?" asked Red Lips, smiling a tiny bit.

"It's for . . . stuff beyond," Thumb Rings said.

"I got a meta-five," Dreadlocks said. "Cost me twenty percent more."

They all cracked up.

"You're all freaks," I said. That cracked them up even more. "I was just saying hello," I told Marilicia. "It's been a while, how are you, all that. But fine, forget it."

"You were not," Marilicia said, her smooth face suddenly serious, eyes squinched tight. "Did you actually expect me to be like, *Oh, really? Really Natasha? You'd do that for me? Help me? So I can maybe come sit with you again?* And if I plot and plan with you, maybe I can wrangle an invitation back to Samesville?"

"I didn't . . . Samesville? What?"

"Because that's the most bruised-up, bottom-of-the-bucket, piece-of-crap peach in the discount store, dude."

"There's no peach! You don't have to get all . . . I was just being nice."

"No you weren't." Marilicia grabbed my arm. "You're never nice, Natasha."

Okay, that pissed me off. I am so sometimes nice.

I shook my arm loose of her grasp and said loud enough for her freak friends to hear, "That's just what you losers tell yourself, to comfort yourself that you don't get to sit with us— *Oh, they're so mean, those popular kids. They're bad and small-minded and cruel.* But you know what? Untrue! Welcome to reality, where you sit here in loser-land because you are too freaking weird to sit with normal people and be happy."

"We are happy," said thumb rings. "And we actually like each other."

"*We actually like each other,*" I imitated, maybe a little louder than I meant to. "My mistake. I thought Marilicia might like to come back to—"

"Wrong," Marilicia interrupted. "Listen. I want you to understand a thing, Natasha. Okay? Six months ago I would've given a vital organ to hear those words from you, the *sorry*, the *you can come back to the Table.*"

"A vital organ?" Dreadlocks asked her.

"Maybe a nonvital organ," Marilicia said, with a laugh in her voice. "A tonsil."

"Gross," Red Lips said. Like she should talk about gross. I think those were tiny dried fish she was eating.

"But you know what I figured out since then?" Marilicia asked.

"What?" I asked, at the same time the cute guy in the blue T-shirt guessed, "You like both your tonsils?"

"That you guys suck," Marilicia said. "All y'all."

"Fine," I said. "See ya."

"No, Natasha, listen." Marilicia stood up and stepped out of the bench. Her tight jeans were tucked into her low boots. She looked good, I had to admit it. She looked, like, comfortable. In herself. She didn't used to, but there she was, looking just, very, Marilicia-like is all I can say. At least her outfit wasn't made of scarves.

"What?" I asked. I let my hair fall around my face, staring down at her cute boots. *I should get boots like that,* I thought. Then I'd have more confidence. My problem is my mom never lets me buy cool shoes.

"Listen," Marilicia said. "You guys? You and those other kids at the Popular Table? You're *boring.*"

"Boring? I wish. I mean, you wish."

"No. Really. You're . . . small."

I let out a chuckle. If there's one thing in the world I am not, it's small—as my skinny little mother has let me know every day of my life. Big like my dad. Taking up too much space. I raised my eyebrows and looked pointedly down at Marilicia. "Small?"

"You know what I mean, Natasha, I know you do," Marilicia whispered. "You're all trying so hard to blend in with each other, to be exactly alike, not left behind, not stand out, not be weird—that you're a wreck. Look how stressed you are. Your hands are fists." She touched my tight hand with her cool fingers.

"I . . ."

"There's an amazing world out there, Tash, and you guys are all hunkered down, squabbling about your little nothing troubles."

I almost smiled when she called me Tash like that. She used to call me Tash. She was the only one, and I really liked it. She started calling me that while we did our experiment about light's effects on plant germination. She made the poster and I collected the data. We were a good team, got an A+ on that and first place in the science fair for sixth graders. We worked so frigging hard on that thing. Then I went to stay with my father for a week and my mother never watered the plants. So they all shriveled up and died before all-county.

I had secretly wished Tash would catch on as my nickname. It just seemed like that would be so cool. I could see myself as Tash, and I'd call Marilicia Ri, and we'd be the leaders of the cool kids. But it didn't catch on and then the plants died, which pissed her off, and she blamed my mom and then she was gone from our table, so that was that.

"Whatever," I said to her, all cold, because why should I care what some Random thinks of me and my friends? I started to walk away. I wanted to get out of the cafeteria and down to the playground before anybody could get the idea I'd been rejected. I expected the freaks behind me to erupt in a good hearty laugh at my expense while I was leaving, but if they did, I didn't hear it.

Losers. I didn't want to sit with them anyway. Thinking they're actually all that? Their parents probably apologize for how peculiar they are, at family parties. I have a cousin like that and her parents are always bragging, *She's so creative.* But what they mean is *She has no friends.* Bunch of weirdos. They just sit together because they were like the Island of Misfit Toys, each from their own unique planet. They weren't even like one another except in all being oddballs.

They were probably just pretending to be happy and like each other. Who wouldn't want to sit at the Popular Table? It didn't even make sense.

Last time I try to reach out and be nice or generous to anybody, I vowed.

Out in the hall I tripped over Truly, who was sitting on the floor like a tight little pretzel.

"Sorry," she said, watching me stumble.

I regained my balance and walked away from her, whispering under my breath so she couldn't hear, "Yeah? Just wait. You will be."

TRULY

NOBODY WAS TALKING to me.

What did I do? Okay, a lot. I know. But not the stuff people were saying online that I did.

I walked the halls between periods. Everybody just watched me until I passed, then turned to whisper behind their hands, behind my back.

If I were brave I'd have gone up the C Stairwell and hid there during lunch. What's the worst they could do to me if I was caught? Suspend me? Please, please, suspend me. Send me home and don't let me come back.

But I was scared, so I sat in the hall, pretending to read until Natasha fake-tripped over me, just to literally kick me while I was down, and then walked away muttering.

I learned nothing. I spent every class doing the math of how many minutes until the end of school when I could go home. I counted backward, ticking off the time during class.

173 minutes. Still 173 minutes. Don't look at the clock again. Ugh, still 173.

172 minutes to go.

172.

Time was stuck. Me, too.

HAZEL

MY PERFECT REVENGE fantasy was coming true: Truly, wandering the halls alone, her huge gray eyes wide and sad. She deserved this, I reminded myself.

Karma.

I even got my smaller, bonus wish of Natasha on the outs, still not back at the Popular Table, though not completely scorned by them anymore either. So, purgatory. I watched her try to get in with Marilicia's group at lunch, but Marilicia clearly said no. Maybe it was partly retribution, which I understand as a powerful primal force and also personally, but I like to think it was also an aesthetic rejection. Natasha was far too ordinary and strivey for Marilicia and her friends. Those kids are *actually* cool.

If I were a world dominator type bad-guy, I'd be laughing my evil cackle, enjoying myself fully because my every wish of misery on my past tormentors was coming true. Just exactly as if I had asked a newly freed genie to do it for me. As if it were all my doing.

But much to my own surprise, I couldn't enjoy it. Couldn't even cackle.

I briefly wondered if maybe I am godlike—able to seek righteous revenge for wrongs done to me but then unable to rejoice at the suffering of my enemies. But no. Sadly, I'm not. If I were, I would have gone over to Truly when she sat all tight in a ball in the hallway during lunch. I didn't. I kept my distance.

Failure of empathy? No. Even worse.

Just a failure of courage on my part.

Honestly? I didn't want to risk being rejected again.

Self-protection.

I spent the rest of the afternoon trying not to notice anybody.

When I got home, my house was empty. My mother had left a note that she and my dad were out for a walk together. Not sure what is going on with them lately. After all these months of fighting, hating each other, and heading, I was absolutely sure, toward a divorce, suddenly they, what? Went back in time and became a high school couple in love again? Can you actually fall back in love with somebody? After you've been really legit mean to each other?

Plus it was like I didn't even exist anymore.

I went out back to sit at the gravesite of my bird for a while to collect my thoughts, and looked again at the photo Brooke had texted me the other day. It was of herself making a silly face.

I hadn't figured out how to respond until right then, at Sweet Pea's gravesite.

I took a photo of myself looking very serious. Over it I wrote: *You shd come over again maybe this time nobody will die.*

After I sent it to Brooke, I started worrying that maybe she wouldn't understand that I was being funny. Or she might think funny weird instead of funny ha-ha. I waited, watching my phone do nothing for a while. I rebooted it a couple times in case it was frozen. Nope. She didn't reply.

I started to text Truly. I knew I should explain what was really going on and my part in it. I should tell her what I'd done and what Natasha had done, including the rumors Natasha was spreading that it was Truly who posted the mean stuff about her. Hard to believe anybody fell for that. So not Truly's style at all. Nobody would believe that about Truly, so she should just stop looking so sad and hurt.

Please stop looking so sad and hurt, I texted her.

But then I deleted it. Soon, I promised myself. I'll text her soon. I'll admit everything and beg her forgiveness. And maybe she'll beg for mine, too.

Maybe I'd even call on the phone, despite my deep phonophobia.

Not quite yet, but soon.

Truly just needs a little time to herself, first, I bargained internally. A person sometimes needs a little time to herself, my dad used to say when I was having a meltdown, time to collect herself, have a little think on things.

Which is exactly what I was doing. With good reason: my parents are acting deeply odd and love-drunk; my best friend dumped me; my other friends bore me. Honestly. There I've said it, they are nice but mostly it's like parallel play punctuated by the occasional *Congratulations on making all-county orchestra—oh thank you so much congratulations on coming in seventh in the chess tournament* oh sweet Jesus kill me now. My dear detested grandmother was just moved to a nursing home, presumably to live forever torturing the nurses there; and my beloved bird was decomposing, buried two feet below where I was sitting alone and ignored in the backyard. Along with the symbols of my earnest and then ironic childhood dreams.

I am way too old to believe that bad things happen precisely *because* I wished a curse onto someone I love. Maybe that's why I can't cackle now.

I'm not sure.

All I know is, all day I kept noticing Truly's attempts at bravery: sad smiles, head held high, hard swallows before giving answers in class. And each time it broke my heart a little.

NATASHA

EVERYBODY DOES IT.

Most of us won't admit it but it's true: each of us wants to be on top, most popular, most powerful, and screw anybody who stands in my way. Some of us do it by blunt force intimidation, like Jack all big and strong, his feet far apart and his arms crossed over his big chest, his posture practically screaming, *don't mess with me.* Some of us do it like Brooke, all Zen calm and accepting, unruffled, like she has plenty of friends already even when she's alone so she doesn't need *you.* Evangeline has her tough-girl scowl and her lightning-fast comebacks, and Lulu has her bubbly nature and solid sense of what's right, plus her tragic family stuff. Clay's got those happy-sad eyes of his, all lost and sweet and needing help.

Marilicia pretends she's not in the game, just like Truly's friend what's-her-face with the green hair—their camouflage is: *It doesn't matter if nobody likes me, I'm so weird I don't care because*

I'm too busy being artsy-fartsy, making ironic comments about people who are way cooler than I could ever hope to be. But I'm obviously a brilliant special snowflake because I have a crap black manicure and look like I got dressed in the dark and brushed my hair with the stick blender.

And then there's Truly. Innocent, sweet Truly, who never even liked me at all, probably. In elementary school, she made me depend on her and then she acted like I was her charity case because my life was less perfect than hers. And then when the tables were turned and I had some power, she couldn't stand that one bit, could she? So she got her revenge. Congrats. She's the most ruthless of us all.

But will any of those people ever admit they're jealous of everybody else? That they spend time every day measuring themselves against every other kid in our grade and falling short, over and over?

No. They won't.

Maybe their parents all coddle them too much. Maybe they all actually believe all the stuff we've been told since we were toddlers about everybody's special and everybody in the class is your friend.

Yeah, right.

You're ordinary. And most of them hate you.

My mom may be a raging bee-yotch to me, but at least she's honest. I can count on her for one thing: she tells it like it is. So? I'm not as smart, not as pretty, not as smooth socially, not ever going to have a shot at being a scientist, not as popular, not as spoiled, not as loved. We don't have a closet full of excess paper goods. So what? At least I know it.

That counts for something.

So when I post stuff about Truly from all my anonymous accounts that take like five seconds each to create, do I feel guilty? Ha. Why should I? My own mom helps me plan out what to say. When I get that twinge in my stomach, I just remind myself, or Mom reminds me, that Truly and her mom would do the same to me in one hot heartbeat. Any of them would. It's all a game. Welcome to the real world.

Stop crying you whiny little wimp, I remind myself, *or you'll be the one on the receiving end. Toughen up and fend for yourself.*

Then I post some more stuff, wacky stuff like a few photos I took of her weeks ago, where she was trying to look all sexy and pretty, with my socks stuffed in the dress I wore to my aunt's wedding. She looks like such a wannabe slut in those, with lipstick smeared across her mouth and her hair flipped over her shoulder. She begged me at the time never to post them or her mom would have a fit. Tough. Bet her mom won't be the only one grossed out by them, either. I'll get that party started in fact.

TRULY

SO MUCH FOR home being a break. All day I counted the minutes, the seconds, until I could come home. But for what? There's no getting away. There's no way to disconnect, not really, not ever. You can decide not to look, but still the vortex spins and catches your life in it, sucks you under, whether you see it happening or not.

You can't break free, ever. That's why they call it the Web, I guess.

I closed my computer. Unplugged it. Didn't work. I was still staring at it.

Just one look, I thought. Let me check one more time. Maybe somebody came to my defense. Or said *lol jk.* One person. One good rope, thrown for me to grab onto and pull myself out of the drowning?

Nope. No rope.

More of the same. More photos barely disguised Natasha put up on sites to rate how ugly I am, how hot or not. Maybe she posted most of the stuff, or maybe other people did a lot too. No way to tell. It hardly mattered anymore, especially with all the strangers and even some kids I definitely knew from school but didn't realize had opinions about me jumping in and judging, rating, criticizing. Looking.

Saying how awful I am, what a terrible person, bad friend, nobody likes me. Why do I bat my eyelashes like such a freak, do I really think boys actually like that? Get over myself. Why do I even come to school when I just annoy everybody by being there all sad-faced and slutty.

On every site. On every app. Faster than I could untag myself.

I didn't even know I knew so many people. Kids I didn't really know were joining in the hate-fest. Cracking jokes, making judgments. A bunch of kids from all-county orchestra think I'm stuck up and not as pretty as I act. A few ninth grade girls think every picture of me deserves a LOL or a SMH. Some boy who doesn't go to school with us and looks sixteen thinks I'm hot. Ew, ew, ew. I couldn't delete myself fast enough, couldn't keep up. I closed my computer, giving up.

I sat down at my desk in front of the stack of History Day scripts I had printed out. I stapled them and neatened the pile. I had already proofread them so many times, I had the whole script memorized, all the parts. *Don't check the phone.* I proofread the script again. Well researched. No mistakes.

I resharpened some pencils. *Don't check the computer again; there's just no point.* I poked the pointy tip of one pencil deep into the central swirl of the fingerprint on my left pointer. I watched it bounce back, almost completely. But it left a tiny mark, a hint of indent. A secret wound. I tried the middle finger, then the ring finger. Tiny, secret scars.

My phone was off, squished between my mattress and box spring. *Don't check it.* But I knew I'd take it out soon. Not just because I'd need to bring it to school in the morning so I could text Mom when I was on my way home and answer "no" when she asked if I was hanging around with my friends. She didn't know how that word, *friends,* didn't apply to me anymore except as a negative—or a weapon.

Tiny, secret scars. Guess I'll have a lot of character.

I flopped down on my bed to stop myself from running to Mom to tell her everything, talk it through, make a plan. It just wouldn't be fair. She has so much to deal with, as it is— her job, of course, but also Henry and Molly. Their problems are so much more real and important.

Me? I'm having trouble with my friends? Boo freaking hoo.

I'm supposed to be the easy one. I'm not brilliant like Henry or hilarious like Molly. I'm easy. That's my whole *thing.* I don't even write in an interesting color ink. I'm just regular. Normal. Easy.

So what am I supposed to do, when I'm none of that?

Cope.

I flipped off the bed to check my phone one last time. Mistake. Big mistake. I threw the phone against my door.

"Ow!" Henry said, out in the hall.

"Are you eavesdropping on me?"

"Yes," he said.

I heard him start to walk away. I ran to my door and opened it. "Want to come in?" I asked him.

"Why?"

"I don't know," I said.

"Want to play a game? I could download—"

"No," I said. "Just, maybe, hang out?"

"Okay," he said. He came in and sat on my desk chair. I sat on my bed. We both looked at our feet.

"I'm not so good at just hanging out," Henry said.

"Yeah, apparently I'm not either."

"Yes you are," he said.

I shook my head and tried not to cry. It didn't work. Oh, great. Another sob attack. I went and closed my door and then sat back down on my bed, still sobbing. When I looked up at Henry, he was just watching me. Sometimes he's hard to be around, but right then he was the best person in the world.

"You're so lucky, Henry," I said.

"At what?" he said.

"Do you, I mean, do you have . . ." I wiped my nose and started over. I didn't want to insult him at all, but I was curious. And Henry doesn't get insulted easily, I reminded myself. Some things bug him a lot but not the things that would hurt most people's feelings. "How's the friend thing going for you this year?"

"Um," Henry said. "There's a kid in my math class who asked me for help on trig."

"What's his name?" I asked.

"Andy," Henry said. "Or maybe Randy. No, Danny. I think."

"Does it bother you?" I asked him. "Not having, like, a group of friends?"

"I don't know," Henry said. "A little, but not very much."

"That's what I mean, you're lucky."

"Oh. I'm not sure that's how I would use the word *luck*."

"Not wanting what you can't have?" I said. "Sounds lucky."

"Luck has to do with chance. I'm not sure you mean lucky."

"Okay." I closed my sore eyes. "My friends hate me."

"Then they aren't your friends," Henry said. "By definition."

"Yeah."

"Maybe you should just forget," Henry said.

"Forget?"

"Forget to think about them. Your ex-friends."

"Yeah?" I asked. "Teach me how I should forget to think."

Henry pondered that for a minute. "It might be like when I tried to teach Mom how to program the TV to record the tennis last year," he finally said. "The gulf between what she understood and where I could start explaining was too wide so I had to just do it for her."

"Oh, well," I said. "Unfortunately that won't work this time so never mind."

We sat there for another few minutes. I blew my nose and

resisted checking my phone, which was having fits over by my door.

"I should just drown that thing in the toilet," I said, more to myself than to Henry.

"In the Watergate scandal," Henry said, "the chief of the burglars was named G. Gordon Liddy."

"Awesome," I said. I knew I should try to be nice despite what everybody clearly thought of me, but I was worn-out. And maybe they were right. Maybe I was just a nasty waste of good oxygen. "Henry, I'm kind of in the middle of a whole lot of—"

"I'm telling you something," Henry said, with the little growl in his voice he sometimes gets. He hates being interrupted.

I flopped back on my bed. "Okay," I surrendered. "The Watergate . . ."

"When Nixon cheated and lied and spied and wrecked his presidency. 1971 to 1973."

I closed my eyes.

"G. Gordon Liddy organized and directed the burglaries at the Watergate. Five of his operatives were arrested inside the Democrats' office there, and the investigation led back to him."

"To G. Gordon," I said, my eyes still closed. Henry didn't require a lot of interaction from the person he was telling his facts to, but his coach had taught him to pause and wait for the other person to say something, every few sentences.

"Yes," Henry said. "To G. Gordon *Liddy*. But when they

questioned him, he wouldn't talk. Wouldn't tell any information. They threatened him all kinds of ways, and tried to make deals with him, but he was unwilling to talk. 'I'm not subject to intimidation,' he told them."

"Cool," I said. "So, Henry, I actually have stuff to—"

"I'm helping you," Henry grunted.

"Okay." Sometimes it's quicker to just let Henry's stories play out.

"G. Gordon Liddy went to jail for fifty-two months instead of talking. He had this party trick he used to do for people," Henry said. "He'd ask for a lighter. A cigarette lighter. He'd light it and hold the flame steady, with his hand right over it, his palm touching the flame. People would be all freaked-out, saying he was burning his own flesh. Which he was. People would have to grab the lighter away to make him stop. And they'd ask him, 'How do you do that? What's the trick?'"

I sat up. "And?" I asked. "What was the trick?"

"The trick is not minding," Henry said. "That's what he told them."

"Not minding that you're burning your own skin off?" I asked.

Henry nodded. "G. Gordon Liddy worked on that trick for a long time. He'd been a scared kid. But he practiced and forced himself to not be scared anymore. Or at least not to mind pain anymore."

"That's sick."

"Yes," Henry said. "And his politics were even sicker. Still,

I thought that might be good advice for you, in your present situation."

"Burn myself up?" I asked.

"No," Henry said, unsmiling. "Try not minding so much."

He watched me until I nodded. "That's good advice."

He stood up and went to my door, stood beside my buzzing phone. "Technically I think you can't drown a phone, because it's inanimate. But I could be wrong about that."

"Thanks, Henry," I said.

"You're welcome," he said and closed my door quietly behind him.

BROOKE

WE MET UP at the wall before school to figure out what to do next. Lulu was scared the principal might get involved, because pretty much the whole school was buzzing about Truly and what had she done and whether everybody should hate her. Rumors were flying that she was a flirt, a fake, a teachers' pet, a liar, and a slut.

She had stopped responding to what people were posting about her online, stopped even untagging herself. I thought that was probably the wise thing. Natasha thought it was practically an admission that it was all true. "Wouldn't you say no, otherwise?" she asked.

We weren't sure.

"Maybe her parents took away her computer," I said. "As a punishment or to protect her. You said they're really strict."

"They are," Natasha agreed.

"I thought it was all mostly just kidding around," Evangeline said. "When did it shift into this mess?"

I looked away from my friends toward the traffic circle. Hazel was getting out of the backseat of a big shiny black car. She slammed the door shut behind her and didn't say good-bye to whoever was driving her. With her head tipped down toward her pile of books, she skulked toward the front door of school, which was a straight line past us. Her hair was dyed blue now, and she had a ring on every single finger, including thumbs.

I reached out and poked Hazel in the back. When she turned around, I crossed my eyes at her, like I had in the selfie I'd sent her. "Hey," I said. "That would be fun."

"What would?"

I could feel Natasha beside me, her hands on her hips, scowling. "What you said," I told Hazel. "Hang out without death or funerals, sometime."

"*Would* it be fun, though?" Hazel asked. "Really?"

"Good point." I laughed. "How about *minimal* death and funerals?"

She smiled. I think it was the first time I've seen her fully smile. Her face actually lit up. I grabbed my bag. "Come on," I said to Hazel. She tilted her head sideways at me, like she was weighing the offer, and then sighed. We walked into the building together.

"You're way weirder than anybody gives you credit for," Hazel said to me as we got to the door. "Including yourself."

"You're probably right," I said. "I need to own it."

"Takes courage," Hazel said.

"Oh, no," I said. "Courage? Forget it." We were passing

my locker but I kept walking with her toward the creepy C stairway, where her locker is.

"Speaking of which," Hazel said. "Did you see the stuff online about Truly?"

"Yeah," I said. "Hard to know what to think."

"She's actually really nice," Hazel said.

"Didn't she basically dump you to be friends with me?" I had to ask.

"She did," Hazel said. "That stung."

"But you're defending her?"

"I've discovered some things about people," Hazel said. "Some difficult truths. My grandmother is dying."

"Oh, I'm so sorry," I said.

"Whoops, we were going for less death," Hazel said. "Whoops."

I laughed a little, but then apologized again.

"No, it's fine," she said and flashed a small smile. "My point was, although I love her, my grandmother is a loathsome woman."

"Oh." None of my friends would ever use the word *loathsome*.

"I can see her flaws, I've realized, and yet have some compassion for her nevertheless."

I nodded. "And, same with Truly?"

"Yes. More, in fact." We stopped walking. Hazel leaned against a locker at the end of the row. "She said a weird thing the other night. Not Truly. My horrid Grandee. In between

criticizing nurses and torturing other patients, she told me
she wanted to give me some advice."

"Uh-oh."

"Exactly. She said I should always try to act a little nicer
than I feel."

I nodded.

"Good advice, right?"

"Yeah, actually," I said. "It is."

"Of course when I asked Grandee why she didn't follow
her own advice, she insisted she did. Which means I guess
she feels even *less* nice than she acts. Which is almost im-
pressive."

I laughed. "She sounds awesome."

"They'll all say *kids these days,* you know."

"Who?"

"The parents, teachers, all of them. The principal."

"When your, sorry, when your grandmother dies?"

"No," she said. "Actually I suspect she'll live forever, out
of spite."

"Oh."

"I mean about the online bullying of Truly. Also of
Natasha."

She unlocked her lock with the tiny key on her shoelace
necklace.

"They'll all be like, 'Kids should stop texting and being
online. Get them off this horrible site or the other horrible
site and everything will be fine.'"

"'They should go outside and play,'" I agreed. "'Wholesome stuff, like when we were kids and everything was good!'"

"Exactly." Hazel dumped all her books into her locker. "But it's not about the social media. It's us. We all suck."

"We do," I agreed.

"My grandmother is a bully about how my mother dresses. My mom is a bully about how my father chews. My dad is impossible about my hair. We didn't invent it. Is my point."

Over at our lockers, my friends were shooting me quizzical looks. What was I doing by C stairs?

"I just thought maybe we were better than that," Hazel said.

"Better than . . . ?"

"Than being nasty to each other about nothing nonsense, just from habit. Or boredom."

"Yeah," I agreed.

"Testing our power," Hazel said. "We think we're being righteous, but . . ."

"Exactly!" I said. "You try to do the right thing, but maybe you end up making the situation worse."

"You didn't," Hazel said. "It's not your fault, what happened after you kicked Natasha out of your lunch table. You were right to do it. That e-mail she sent Truly was cruel."

"How . . . wait, how did you know . . ."

"I'd rather not say for now, if you don't mind," she said.

"I'll tell you eventually, I swear on Sweet Pea's memory. But for today let's just say a lot of this is my fault."

"Yours?" I asked. "No way. You're completely an innocent bystander, here."

"No," she said. "Far from. But, if I could ask one favor of you?"

"Sure," I said. "What do you need?" My mind was spinning.

"Get everybody to ease up on Truly. She doesn't deserve the pummeling she's getting. Well, nobody does. Probably not even Natasha, though I'd steer clear of her for sure. But the rumors about Truly flirting with the boys? Including Clay? All lies. I swear. And she never posted one mean thing about Natasha."

I nodded. "I believe you. I'm not sure what I can do, but—"

"Golda Meir once said, 'Don't be humble; you're not that great.'"

"I like that."

"You have power around here, Brooke. Don't deny it. You can tip the dynamic a little toward kindness."

"Follow your grandmother's advice?"

She nodded. "Especially if you wear a scarf."

What? "Um, okay."

"Thank you."

"I mean, I'll try."

"I know."

"Hey, Hazel?"

"Yes?"

"Did Sweet Pea ever come to you in a dream, to fly?"

"Not yet," Hazel said, flashing that full-face-illuminating smile again, for a millisecond. "But hope, like my grandmother, springs eternal."

CLAY

I WALKED OUT of math first period hating myself. I had done all the homework, for real. I didn't look up the answers until after, and then worked through why I got them wrong until I understood them. In a movie of my life, I'd rock the quiz today, right? After the montage of me sitting at the kitchen counter and at my desk, on my bed, on my floor, frigging wrestling algebra to the mat? I wasn't distracted by the Internet even once. It's true. My parents made sure of that. But still, I didn't give up. I didn't decide, *Screw them, if they think taking away my stuff will make me get better grades I'll show them the opposite is true.* Well, I considered that. But I went the other way. I worked my butt off. But still when I turned over the paper on my desk for the math test this morning? Bzzz. None of it looked even familiar. Thanks for playing.

So I wasn't looking where I was going, is why I almost bumped into Brooke. She grabbed me by the sweatshirt sleeve and dragged me toward the C stairwell. "What's wrong?" I asked her. "Besides basically every answer I just . . ."

She was yanking me up the stairs toward the locked door of the third floor, where we're completely not allowed to go.

"Hey," I said. "You okay?" She was breathing fast, her chest going up and down. I forced my eyes away because I didn't want to be a goon, but man, it was not easy because, seriously, she was making me feel all kinds of weird.

"What's *up?*" I asked.

"Did you . . ." Brooke leaned against the wall. "Have you seen Truly?"

"Sure," I said. "Wasn't she in math just now?"

"Yes. Did you see how pale she looked, and, like, haunted? Everybody needs to take a step back, don't you think? Ease up on her? Stop spreading lies about her?"

"Jack told me about that," I said. "He said it was all lies, too."

"I know it is," she said. "Are you not online at all?"

"They took away my phone," I admitted. So humiliating. "And my computer."

"So you weren't texting with Truly last night?"

"I've never texted with her in my life!"

"So then what were—"

"You don't have to believe me, but I totally studied last night. I did. And then, well, I don't see how I could get above a fifty on that quiz. And that's if she gives *show your work* credit and likes the little extra where I wrote down the definition of algebra. Do you know what *algebra* means?"

"I don't care," Brooke said.

"Me neither. Davidson hates me. And I'm obviously an idiot, no matter how much I study. After this, my parents are gonna take away my, I don't know. Bed. Pants. Arm."

She shook her head. "You should ask your dad to go for a run with you."

"Right. For company? How much of a loser am I? He doesn't even run—"

"A fever," she said. "I know. But, like, you could say, here's something easy for me, but it's hard for you. And then you could be like, studying for me is like running for you. It doesn't come easy. I'm trying but it's hard. And then maybe he'll get it."

I couldn't say anything. I just stood there, where we weren't allowed to be, and if we got caught we'd be suspended. I'd get drop-kicked out of my family for sure if that happened. But there was not one spot on earth I wanted to be instead of right there in the pee-stinking dark C Stairwell landing, with Brooke. She got it. She got *me*. Not that I'd be asking my dad to come run with me anytime soon, though the image of that was hilarious. Just, yeah. How does she just *know* . . . but she was still talking and I'd lost track again.

"It started out like normal stuff, joking around," Brooke was whispering. "And then it got bad, fast. Really bad. And the thing is, I think it's actually at least partly my fault."

"Your fault?"

Brooke nodded. "Despite what Hazel just said, which was so confusing, because . . ."

As she talked a voice inside my head was grunting, *Grab her grab her.* Which was completely weird and inappropriate. I was like, *Shut up stupid caveman grunty voice! What would I even do if I grabbed her? Like, knock her down? Hug her?* The voice ignored me and just kept grunting, *Grab her grab her!*

So meanwhile I was forgetting to pay attention to what my very upset best friend who never gets upset about anything was saying at all.

". . . was the right thing to do, but maybe it wasn't," she finished.

"So wait," I said, trying to focus. "What exactly did you do wrong?"

"I was trying to shut down the Drama, and I think I made it worse. Clay . . ."

"What? I was listening!"

"Do you think I'm . . . weird?"

"Deeply," I said.

She stared at me. I thought maybe she was going to punch me. But instead she put her hands on my waist. "Thank you," she whispered.

Then she pulled me close and kissed me full on the mouth. *What?!*

Her lips were so soft. I took my hands out of my sweatshirt pockets where they'd been lodged like a couple of rocks between us and circled Brooke's back with my arms. Pulled her closer. Kept kissing.

I guess she's the one who pulled away because I seriously

would've stayed there kissing her until spring, without coming up for air or even a sandwich.

"Wow," I said.

"I don't know if you like me, that way," she said. "And we're friends, which I don't want to wreck, but I, the thing is?"

"Brooke . . ."

"I like you," she said. "Like, *that way*. So. There it is. And, so, whatever. I'm owning it. You can say no. Of course. And we'll just, that's fine. It'll be weird and then it won't or maybe it'll always—"

"Brooke," I interrupted.

"What?"

"I do like you. I've . . . yeah. Me, too."

"Oh," she said. "Okay, then."

We didn't know what to do then, either of us, so we just stood there awkwardly until finally I said, "We should, um . . ."

"Yeah," she said. So we started down the stairs. We were late for social studies and of course my math problems were still a bunch of broken parts, unreunioned. But my fingers brushed against Brooke's as we rushed down the steps, so for at least that one second, maybe a bunch more, everything felt really incredibly okay about my entire . . . situation.

NATASHA

I WENT STRAIGHT to the back corner of the social studies classroom to sit down with my group. None of them looked up at me. I slumped in my chair and took out my notebook. I wasn't sure if I was back in for lunch and in general, or what Truly's status was, but we were definitely stuck together for one more day at least, because of stupid History Day.

Brooke dashed in all flushed and smiley, a minute after the bell, apologizing. Clay was right behind her, grinning. Were they gossiping about me out in the hallway or something? Neither of them would even look my way.

Truly pulled a stack of typed, stapled packets out of her bag and handed them out to us without a word.

"Wow," Brooke said. "Truly, this is . . . Thanks for doing all this."

We all started reading.

"There are only four parts," Evangeline said, flipping pages.

Truly nodded. She had a script on the desk in front of her, neat, pages unturned. She'd written the whole thing and none of us had even done any of the research to help. But she'd put all of our names up top, her own last.

Now watch, they'll all think she's so awesome for that, when they should be concentrating on all the bad stuff about her. Focus.

"Who's not in it?" Lulu asked Truly.

"Me," Truly whispered.

"You're directing?" I asked. Of course, she'd made herself the boss. Typical.

"I'm nothing," Truly answered.

Truly was contracting on the chair. She looked like one of the caterpillars in the butterfly hatching kit I had once, when they started entering the chrysalis stage. Tight and hard. Then most of them died.

"So wait. This Peggy girl?" Lulu pointed at me. "She totally played Benedict, right?"

"Hold up, I'm still trying to read this," Evangeline said. "Am I a traitor or not?"

"Yes, you are, Benedict," Truly mumbled. "But nobody here is completely innocent because . . ."

"Yes!" Lulu shouted. "Exactly!" Lulu gets very psyched when she figures stuff out. Focus, Lulu. Remember what we were just discussing about Truly and how evil *she* is?

Lulu bounced in her seat. "So Benedict wants to turn over West Point to the Brits. But meanwhile it was Natasha!" She pointed her stubby finger at me.

"Wait," I said. "Why am I the—"

"Natasha totally masterminded this whole thing, and then she, like, collapses on the floor when Brooke comes in!" Lulu said. "In a big fake fit! Natasha just pretends to be completely innocent when it's all her fault!"

"Well, it's not *all* her fault," Truly said from inside her cocoon.

I was trying to speed-read through the script, but it was hard to concentrate because I was trying to figure out if everything they were saying had double and triple meanings and if they were actually attacking Truly or it was me they were turning on again. My stomach was churning.

Leave it to Truly to get everybody back on her side with a stupid school project.

"I'm starting to get confused about who to feel sorry for," Lulu said.

"Preach," I agreed.

"Well, you're the worst," Evangeline said. I looked up.

She was staring at me.

"Me?" I asked.

Evangeline slammed her palms onto her desk. "I should fully divorce your butt." Oh, shoot me. She was actually talking about the freaking script? What is wrong with everybody?

"He'd never divorce her," Truly said. "Even if he knew she was cheating on him with the French guy. And not just because it wasn't that common back then. He couldn't believe somebody so charming and beautiful and popular as Peggy

240

would ever be with him. He felt completely unworthy all the time. Which maybe explains some stuff he did. He felt so desperate and, like, inadequate, it made him just forget to think. He knew he was hard to get along with," Truly said quietly. "He was really smart but kind of, anti-charming?"

"I like that," Brooke said. "Anti-charming. That's awesome."

"Only George Washington really liked him," Truly said. "And then Benedict betrayed him."

"What a fungus," Lulu said. "Betraying your best friend?"

Truly shrugged.

"Yeah," I said, raising my eyebrows. "Who would do a nasty thing like that?"

"He had this idea he could maybe be a hero," Truly said. "John André—the French guy—put the idea in his head that maybe he, this big ugly rough guy nobody liked, no social skills, anti-charming . . . Maybe he could turn West Point over to the British and end the war and everybody would hail him as a hero."

"*Hail* him?" I started to mock, but they were all looking at Truly, into it, so I stopped. My stomach made a loud embarrassing gurgling noise.

Maybe nobody heard though because Truly kept talking: "Benedict thought, maybe if he did this, this one maybe questionable thing, he could be even cooler and more beloved than George Washington. So he took a chance and did it. And then he got caught and had to run away, like a rat through the woods, and he lived the rest of his life in England."

"Wait, he got away?" Lulu asked. She flipped to the end of the script. It was five pages long. "They didn't catch him? I thought they killed him."

"Nope," Truly said. "They tried, but he survived. He lived a long time, after that. He died an old man. And his dying words were about how he wished he'd died with his friends on the battlefield."

Nobody said anything. Around the room the low murmur of other groups discussing their projects burbled. Our group had ground to a stop.

"That's sad," Evangeline said, after a full minute.

Come on, people. "He betrayed his only friend," I reminded her. "Doesn't get any lower than that."

"Still," Brooke said. "He made some bad choices, sure, but, like, you can see somebody's flaws and still have compassion for them"

"Maybe to be a hero," I said, "you just have to die before everybody finds out the truth about you."

"Yeah," Truly whispered. "Maybe."

"I mean, obviously it's just a first draft and it's kind of a muddled mess. So it's hard for any of us to really know what you're trying to say here," I told Truly. "But maybe you mean that if a person realizes he or she has been a betraying, lying, conniving douche, who doesn't even know how to be a decent friend? It would be better for that person to just go ahead and die."

Truly stood up. Pale and shaking, she stood there for a few seconds and then walked right out of the class.

After the door closed behind her, everybody turned and stared at me, like it was my fault.

"What?" I asked. "I was just saying."

The bell rang a few seconds later. We all collected our stuff, shoved our scripts into our bags. Nobody said I should join them, I could sit at their table. My mom had been so sure they'd grab me right back in, once we exposed Truly. Everything would be normal again.

But nothing was.

I went to the girls' room, locked myself in a stall, and texted my mom. So pathetic, I know. But who else could I text?

I did what you said, head high, no mercy. Truly just walked out of school. I'm a little worried about her. Maybe I was too mean?

I sat there on the disgusting toilet with my pants up, trying not to touch anything. Waiting.

Stay strong! Mom texted back.

I'm trying, I typed quickly with my thumbs. And then added: *I'm just not sure what STRONG would be, now, though.*

TRULY

JUST KEEP WALKING, Butterfly.

Don't think.

Don't feel.

Don't decide anything.

Just walk.

HAZEL

URGENT—CALL ME. Seriously, Truly—answer your phone, your texts, your e-mail.

Come on, Truly. Answer. I have to tell you some stuff about what's been going on. You don't know. It's my fault. Mine and also Natasha's, the two people you've ever thought of as best friends.

Okay you never cut school in your life before, so this is freaking me out. You never even faked being sick, unlike for example every other kid in the world. So this is really weird and hyperdramatic, for you.

And I am the one who is supposed to be weird and hyperdramatic. Stop taking my part hahahaha.

I'm thinking of stopping that, btw. Maybe trying to be more normal. Or at least not trying so hard to be the weird kid. But that's a story for another day. For now PLEASE ANSWER.

Truly?

Please, Truly.

Please connect.

TRULY

STANDING BY THE side of Big Pond.

Never been this close to it before. I'm not allowed, so I never even thought about stepping off the sidewalk toward it, never mind down the hill.

I can't see my reflection in the murky water.

My fingertips are cold on my buzzing phone.

Last thing I need is to read any more of the truth about how horrible I am, posted everywhere. So I don't bother to look at it. I just look down into the bottomless murky water.

What did I do?

Why are they all so mad at me?

I haven't been a great friend, or a good person. I know that. I've messed up and been awkward and selfish. I'm too sensitive. I was so excited at the thought of becoming popular that I forgot to think. I left my best friend, Hazel, hanging alone. I wasn't sensitive enough to what Natasha was going through, and maybe I enjoyed the attention the boys were paying to me too much. I don't know how to be cool.

But if the choice in life is either having no friends, or handing over power to your friends to hurt you, I'm not sure how you decide. Both options stink.

I knew when Mom and Dad got home they'd be so mad— the school sends out robocalls or alerts, supposedly, when a kid cuts. Which I did. So I was stalling, here at Big Pond Their star, their easy kid, the good one. Yeah, well. Sorry. Blew that, too.

I flipped through some apps on my phone. More of the same. People were about evenly split between saying gross positive stuff and gross negative stuff. I was madly pointlessly untagging myself when I got a text from Hazel, the first since that day I walked away from her at our lockers: *URGENT— CALL ME.*

I ignored it. She probably just wanted to join in on the fun of hating me. She was the one person I deserved it from most. But I had all those photos to find and untag.

Another text: *Seriously! Please Truly. I have to tell you something . . .*

I ignored that one, too. That the photos of me look all slutty and stupid? Yeah, thanks Hazel. Seen 'em. You have every right to hate me, but I seriously can't take it on right now. I'm too busy deleting myself, bit by bit.

A bunch more texts from Hazel, which I ignored/deleted until this one:

I know you're seeing this, Truly—and you don't have to respond if you don't want to but I have something really important I need to tell you. And everybody; I'll tell everybody it was me if you want me to. But I want to tell you first. I need . . .

I closed my eyes and took a breath, my phone cold and heavy as a gun in my hand. I was so tired. She needs . . . what?

Maybe something happened with her parents, or her brother, or her grandmother?

But what could I possibly do for her? Or for anyone? I was like the opposite of Midas—everything I touch turned to . . .

Another buzz.

Please, Hazel texted. *Truly—I'm sorry. I didn't mean . . . ugh. It's too long to explain by text. If I e-mail you something, will you please open it?*

There was just nothing left in me. I wasn't thinking about whether to say yes or no, wasn't wondering what could possibly be making Hazel push her own drama onto me right at that worst moment of my entire life. I wasn't doing anything. I couldn't even muster the necessary grace to say, *I'm the one who should be apologizing, Hazel—you have nothing to be sorry for!*

I knew that's what I needed to do. My mom says when you feel down, the best strategy is to find a way to be kind to someone else. Here it was, presenting itself to me, a chance to be kind to someone who completely deserved my apology and kindness.

But I didn't text her back an apology. I didn't text her back at all. I didn't even do that one small good thing. I just stood there, feeling the wind blow around instead of through me, wondering what right I even had to make those air molecules change their paths.

Then this text came through from Brooke: *Hey. Why'd you cut? Are you coming to Evangeline's to rehearse after school?*

No, I texted back. Why would I answer Brooke and not Hazel? Because she's popular and despite everything I still feel buzzy when her name shows up on my phone?

Don't let Natasha get to you, Brooke texted.

It's not just Natasha, I texted back fast. *It's everybody. Including me.*

As soon as I hit SEND on that to Brooke, this text came through from Hazel:

> If you want to hate me forever I won't blame you but first know this:
> 1. everybody screws up sometimes
> 2. especially in middle school
> 3. I love you
> 4. Please sign into your e-mail and then immediately change your password because locker143542 is not secure
> 5. But who really is?

What was she even blathering on about?

My hand clenched the phone tighter, tighter, my one life-line to everybody, this phone I begged my parents to buy me for my thirteenth birthday, back when becoming a teenager seemed like it would be so great, so exciting and full of adventure.

Hahahahaha.

I threw my phone up into the air. I watched it arc perfectly through the air, like a Salugi ball thrown by Evangeline, or Jack, one of the kids who is actually coordinated. It sliced silently through the unbelievably blue sky and then crashed into the water in the center of the pond. Not an explosion. Barely disturbed the pond water, never mind the universe. Just a quiet *plink*.

And it was gone.

JACK

I WALKED OVER to Truly's house instead of going to practice. I didn't care. Coach could bench me. He'd be right to. I was letting the team down, cutting practice, I knew. Sometimes you have to do the wrong thing, though.

You just do.

She lived a long way from school, I knew. I had looked her up in school directory. Not in a creepy stalker way, just . . .

Okay maybe that does seem creepy stalker of me. I was looking up her phone number because I was going to call her to ask *What was the science homework* but I hung up before anybody answered because, yeah.

But I am pretty good at memorizing things like her phone number and her address. And walking. I can just walk and walk; it's no problem.

I rang the doorbell at her house. Nobody answered. I knew she had left school early, I watched her walk out and off school grounds, watched her walking toward home, so I knew it wasn't that she'd stayed after school hanging out with friends or doing sports or anything.

I rang a few more times. No answer. I was about to start knocking and yelling but then I heard a squeak from around back. I stayed very still, listening for another sound. One little squeak. Then another, each followed by a dull little thump.

I went down the steps and around past the garage onto the narrow side path. When I got to the backyard, I saw her, sitting on a swing in the wooden swing set back there, slowly swaying.

I didn't want to startle her so I walked with heavy steps toward her. She lifted her eyes slowly to see me and didn't scream or jump, so I kept going.

When I got to the swing set I wasn't sure if I should maybe give her some pushes like a little kid, which is what she looked like, or just sit down in the other swing. I went with sit on the other swing. It seemed like the better choice.

I pushed a bit with my toes, but kept them in the dirt, dragging, catching up to Truly's rhythm.

After about a million minutes of silence, I thought of something to say: "How's your busted knee?"

She shrugged one shoulder. "Okay."

"The stitches came out fine?"

She nodded a tiny bit.

"So it's healing up well?"

"Crusting over."

I nodded. "Sorry again about smashing into you."

"Oh, no," she said. "I didn't mean to—I wasn't . . ."

And then she started bawling. Seriously. Not a few little tears tracking down her cheeks like used to happen to my mom sometimes back in Ohio when she thought I was asleep. No—this was full-out sobs, with her shoulders shaking and her nose running so much she had to wipe it on her sweatshirt sleeve. I didn't know what to do. I had no tissues. My mom tries to give me a travel pack sometimes but I never take it. So I had nothing.

Well, not nothing.

I leaned forward and reached into my backpack. "Here," I said, handing her the small white box with its slightly crushed ribbons.

She didn't take it. She was still sobbing. Her shoulders were heaving and wet was dripping from her face to the dirt. Mostly tears, I think, but there might have been snot and drool in there, too.

Why didn't I take those tissues?

"Oh, wait," I said. "I have a napkin. Don't worry it's clean. My sandwich today was kind of dry, not my best effort— turkey with not enough honey mustard and some Craisins. Eh. But on the plus side, I didn't use the napkin. So you're in luck."

I had fished it out by then and held the napkin under her face, which was parallel to the mud puddle fast forming between her tiny feet.

She took my napkin and rubbed it on her face.

First time I ever felt happy about a too-dry sandwich.

She sniffed a bunch of times and then said, "Thanks."

I was still holding the box. I reached it out so she could see it better. "This is for you," I said. "Maybe it will cheer you up."

She shook her head slightly, or maybe she just was sitting there and the swing bobbled a little.

"Do you want me to open it for you?" I asked.

Maybe she was too shy to say she did want me to open it for her, yes please. Or maybe she was thinking, Why is this guy being a creeper and bringing me a present? Like my mom hinted she would, though Mom thought we were talking about a possible present, not an actual one. Still, my mom is very smart about reactions, and normally I would never ignore her advice. But it was too late by then to have not bought it, so I decided to just keep it tucked into my backpack where nobody putting away socks would notice it accidentally.

And now it was also too late to not show it to Truly.

"Or you could open it," I suggested. "When you're ready. No rush."

"Who's it for?" she asked.

"You," I said.

She plucked it gently from my hand. Then she just held it for a while. The ribbons were crushed in multiple places. I wished they looked as smooth as when I first got them. I wished she would open it. She was just holding it, still.

"It's not my . . . why?"

"I just wanted to," I said.

"Did you see what they said about me online?" she asked.

"Yeah," I said. "Some."

"Oh, no," she moaned.

"People say a lot of stupid and untrue stuff. What are you gonna do?"

She leaned forward and carefully lifted the box off my hand. Her bony little fingers began working those knots open. I had spent a bunch of my free time picturing that exact thing, so much, in fact, that it was like I was remembering it, even while I was watching it happen for the first and only time right in front of me.

She dropped the ribbons into her lap and lifted the box top off, then fished the bracelet out. It didn't look as pretty as I remembered from the shop. It looked like maybe I made it out of tin foil scraps.

"It's for you," I said. "It's a bracelet."

She looked up at me suddenly, the gray parts of her eyes floating in pools of red. It was a tiny bit scary. She held the bracelet up and looked at it. *Please think it's pretty,* I was thinking. *Please don't think I'm a creepy stalker.*

I was imagining that she'd maybe put it on, asking for my help if she wanted it, and then maybe shyly smile and thank me. And then maybe we could swing a while, talking about this and that.

That's how I was thinking it should go.

But instead she just sat still, with the bracelet dangling limply off her finger.

"I got it for you a while ago," I explained. "After I knocked you down at Salugi. I was waiting for a good time to . . . but then I saw you leave school early today, and I know all that stupid stuff people posted, so I thought, maybe you could use a present."

She looked down at the bracelet dangling like a spiderweb from her fingers, then back at me. "Why are you so nice to me?" she whispered.

"I like you," I admitted.

She shook her head.

"It's true," I said. "I mean I know I don't know you that well, but I've noticed you for a long time. I liked your bug-poop-in-dust report. Also your gravelly voice and how smart and good a person you are, and—"

"No," she interrupted. "I'm not good. I'm petty and selfish and I threw my phone in Big Pond just now."

"Why?"

"Because I'm just wrecked."

"Wrecked meaning your busted knee?" I asked. "Because that's my fault."

"No, like, my personality," she said.

"Your personality seems good to me," I said.

"It's not," Truly said.

"Maybe you're just, kind of like that bracelet," I said, wishing she would please put the bracelet on instead of leaving it dangling limply like that. "Delicate, a little bit. Most of us are, no matter how sturdy we look, I think. So maybe we all have to be, you know, a little gentle with each other. Less rough. But maybe it's also stronger than it seems so don't worry too much about that."

She blinked a few times. Some teardrops were caught in her eyelashes.

"I don't know a lot about bracelets or girls, though, so I could be wrong," I admitted.

"Thank you, Jack," she said.

"So you want help putting it on?"

"Okay," she said, and held out her hand to me. I managed to open the bracelet's clasp on my third try and stretched the bracelet around her tiny pale wrist. Then it took another few tries to open the clasp again and hook it inside the tiny silver O. But I did it, my thick thumbs managed.

Truly waggled her hand a bunch of times. The bracelet twinkled in the sunlight while she did it. It didn't fall apart in confetti bits on the dirt, luckily, because that would have been really bad for a couple of reasons, including that I had just basically compared her to the bracelet. So, phew on that.

She let her hand hang down by her side. The bracelet looked just like I'd hoped it would, sparkly and pretty on her wrist.

"If you don't like it, you can return it and choose something else," I said, not taking my eyes off it.

"I like it a lot," she said.

"It's not too . . . flimsy?"

"The opposite," she said. "It feels strong as a rope to me, actually."

"Okay," I said, hoping she meant it in a good way. I stood up from the swing. "A rope?"

"Yeah."

"You like rope?"

She smiled a little. She has such a sweet smile. "I've actually been wishing for one to grab on to."

"Oh. Okay. Good then. Well, I guess that's all. I just, I wanted you to have that. It's not real rope, which, if I'd known you wanted it, I guess I could've . . . and it's no watermelon lollipop but . . ."

She laughed. I hadn't heard her laugh full-out before. It had kind of a bubbling-over quality, like when you're heating milk and it gets all frothy.

"It's perfect," she said. "Thank you."

"Phew," I said. "Well, then, see you tomorrow, bye."

I live far from Truly, the other side of town, the less fancy area, but a long walk wasn't going to hurt me any. Very little could right then. I'm strong. I got through people saying no to me before this; I could get through a girl wearing a bracelet I bought her and saying it was perfect, thank you. Even if my face might explode from smiling so hard as I walked along. Even if I might have to run partway home because of so much energy booming inside me.

One foot in front of the other, my mom says, that's how you get through stuff—keep going. Keep going, I told myself, smooth and steady; don't jump around or shout *YES!* Not until you're out of sight of Truly's house and then a few blocks more to be safe. I calmed myself down by thinking about what to make for dinner. Maybe something new, something with multiple steps and lots of ingredients. I had enough energy in me to make a ten-course meal. Something delicious, and when she's done Mom would say, "Oh, Jack, thank you. This is so good."

And it would be.

BROOKE

WHEN I GOT home from Evangeline's after school, my dad was standing in the kitchen, staring at groceries. He had spread them all over the counters in piles and groups instead of putting them away straight from the bags, the way my mother does. His way drives her nuts. She has to leave the kitchen when he unloads groceries. He gets it done but it takes forever, my mom complains. They have such different styles and speeds it's kind of funny they could work together all those years in the bookstore and also at home, always together. Though, of course, their store was as belly-up as Hazel's dead bird, now, so maybe it wasn't such a successful partnership after all.

"What are you doing, Dad?" I asked him.

"Hmmm?"

I leaned against the fridge with him, crossed my arms like him. "Why are we admiring the groceries?"

He laughed his snort-laugh. "I just spent two hundred

dollars in the grocery store," he said. "I came home with all this but no milk, which is what we needed."

"Oops," I said.

"And I was just thinking, I once spent two hundred dollars on a car."

"Really? Two hundred bucks for a whole car?"

"Yup," Dad said. "Well, it had no floor. And no brakes."

"Oh."

"But I was young," he said, sighing. "And it was a car. And I had places to go and no need yet for a floor, or milk, or brakes."

"You miss it?" I asked him. "That car and, that . . . feeling?"

"Nah," he said. "Other than the lack of milk, I'm the happiest guy I know."

"Yeah, but, what about . . . you know, all the bad stuff that's happening?"

"Bad stuff's gonna come," Dad said. "You just have to walk it off and start over, when it does."

"Sure, but what if you're the one who blew it?"

"Everybody's that one sometimes, darlin'," Dad said. "I figure, you go all out, shoot the moon, every time. Sometimes you get lucky. And meanwhile you work on developing a good second move for when you mess up. If you never fail, you're not trying hard enough. That's my strategy. For what it's worth."

"Mine, too," I said. "I think. I'm trying, anyway."

"Then good luck to you. You're gonna need it. Now help

me put all this crap away before your mother gets home and sees what a mess I've made."

While I was helping I got a Snapchat from Clay. It was a photo of the C stairwell. Over it he'd written, *"Best place on earth."*

I managed to save it, just in time.

NATASHA

I WAS STUCK.

It was a tight squeeze getting into the dress, but I had forced it on. I had told them all I was definitely wearing it tomorrow for the performance, so it had to work. It had to. They were all mad at me enough already, for being harsh to Truly at school and then she went missing. I told them she sometimes gets emotional and not to worry but I don't know if they believed me until we saw she deleted a bunch of stuff and answered Brooke's text. So at least she wasn't dead or anything. They still all seemed mad, though.

Could I really have grown so much since my aunt's wedding? No way. The dress must've shrunk. I somehow worked it down over my body and checked myself out in the mirror. I looked like a cartoon character. Or maybe a sausage. It was horrible. And I hadn't even zipped it yet! This wasn't going to work, obviously. I started peeling it off, from the bottom up. My mother didn't have any dresses I could steal because the woman is way skinnier than I am. As she lets me know, even without saying so, every time she glances at me.

It had already been a long afternoon, when we were supposed to be practicing our play at Evangeline's, but instead we basically spent the whole time online looking for Truly and making sure she was okay. And then deleting or blocking all the mean stuff about her everywhere.

Ugh. Can nothing work for me? Ever?

I was sweating. I was taking the dress off over my head and it was really freaking tight. Maybe Mom washed it, or took it in to prank me. Or somehow when Truly tried it on that afternoon she came over and the two of us hung out laughing so much, maybe the dress had somehow squooshed down to her tiny proportions.

Obviously that was impossible. The dress was cutting off blood flow to my brain. I had gotten it partway off. I had to stop to catch my breath and reassess my strategy.

The dress was inside-out over my chest, head, and arms. It was so freaking dark. I hate overhead lights and I didn't need it bright as an operating room to check myself out in the mirror in a dress I was worried might be a squeeze, thank you. But with the dress inside-out over my head in the lowest dimmed click of lamplight of my room, I couldn't see anything.

Okay, it was time to admit the truth: I was completely trapped in the torture-chamber-tube of dress, and my fingers were starting to prickle, up there in the air like *Hey, throw me the football.*

I bent over so my hands touched my rug and tried to step onto the hem of the dress with my toes. It wasn't working. I chased the bottom of the dress (which was almost at my fingertips) around with my feet. Folded in half like that I lost track of where I was and crashed into my night table. So there went my lamp, smashing onto the floor in shards of glass. In case it wasn't dark enough before.

"You okay?" Mom called out in the hall.

"Fine!" I yelled back.

"What are you doing in there?"

"Nothing!"

"Did you just throw your lamp against the wall?" she demanded. "Because so help me, Natasha, I have had just about enough of your—"

"No!" I yelled. Oooh, I was fully sweating.

Her phone rang. I could hear it perfectly well. Was she like leaning against my door? What is *wrong* with her?

"Oh, hello, Alicia," Mom said. Alicia? That's Truly's mom. Why was she calling my mother while I was trapped in my dress?

I'm fine, Mom was saying. *You? Oh, really? No I didn't know that. Sorry to hear she's . . . Humph, Truly always seemed so even-keeled . . . Uh-huh. I for one try to stay out of . . . uh-huh. Ugh, kids these days, I tell you, the screens! It's constant! And the . . . oh. No, I didn't hear that. I'm not sure why you think I would have anything to do with . . . Uh-huh. I am listening, Alicia, but did it occur to you that maybe you're only getting one side of the . . . I know that. Yes. Who said? I don't know anybody named Hazel. Hazel? Oh, that kid. Well, she's obviously a paragon of sanity, that one. She said what? Why do you trust her word over mine, then? What proof? Well, but, uh-huh but maybe Truly posted some nasty stuff about Natasha, too. Did you think of . . . These things have two sides, at least, and you're only . . . Uh-huh. Uh-huh. I don't see why it's Natasha's fault if Truly throws her phone in the . . . was Natasha even there? Right, so how is this . . . Are you suggesting . . . Well, there I agree with you. You bet. And you keep Truly away from . . . Hello? Hello?*

"Natasha! Open the door this minute!" Mom yelled, banging on it. "Or so help me I will kick it off the hinges. Natasha, don't test me I will do it!"

I shuffled to the door still trapped inside the dress. On the way I guess I stepped on some glass shards that used to be my lamp. "Ow ow ow," I was saying as I bent in half to unlock my door. My mother slammed the door open and it swung into my arm-and-head enclosing dress and knocked me over onto my butt. "Ow!"

"What are you *doing*?" my mother demanded, flicking on the overhead. Great.

I lifted my arms enough so I could see her face through the dress/periscope. "Just hanging," I said.

"Just . . . have you lost your mind?"

"Are my feet bleeding?"

"Yes! And you are going to rip that dress. Why are you always such a disaster?" She sat down on my bed, cross-legged. "That lamp cost eighty dollars. And unlike Truly's family . . . that was her mother on the phone just now. Do you know what Truly did today?"

"Cut school," I said. "Could you . . . Mom? I can't. . . ."

"She tossed her phone in Big Pond. And her mother wants me to tell you to stay away. Like it's my kid who's going mental."

"I'm hemorrhaging from my feet and trapped vertically in a dress," I said through the tunnel of dress. "Truly's mom could make a pretty strong case, I think."

"Good point."

We both started to laugh. A little at first, but then the whole thing just, I don't know. It all seemed so nuts. I rested my hands on my bed so I wouldn't topple over onto the glass again. Mom and I could not stop laughing. I ended up on my knees beside the bed, like a little kid saying her prayers, by the time we got a hold of ourselves. A few aftershocks of laughing shook us as we sighed it out.

"So, what *are* you doing?" Mom asked finally.

"I can't get out of this dress," I said, laughing a little more. "Can you help me?"

"I don't know how," she said.

I swallowed hard. The laughs disappeared. *She didn't know how to help me.* "I need you to know how."

"But . . ."

"Just try something," I whispered. "Please be able to."

She tugged and yanked and pulled. She dragged me onto the bed. I stepped on more glass shards and banged my shin on the bed frame, but little by little and then all at once I was out. I blinked in the air.

"Ugh, that was like childbirth," my mother said, gawking

at my nearly naked, sweaty body. "Never planned to birth you a second time at age thirteen."

"Ew," I said, wrapping my arms around myself.

"Oh, Natasha, look at you."

"No!" I yelled. "Don't look at me. I'm fat and sweaty and I don't want to hear it, okay?"

"Natasha, I never said you —"

"Yes, you did," I said. I was shaking, my fists clutched in front of my face. "You always do. You make me hate myself, and then, it's like, all I am is hate. All I have, all I can put out there into the world is hate." I was thumping my fists into my forehead.

Mom's face looked shocked, maybe hurt, maybe mad. I didn't know and didn't care. "You're gonna blame me for every sorry thing in your life?" she asked.

"Hurt people hurt people you once said," I yelled at her. "Well, you must be in agony because look what you do to me. And make me do to my friends."

"Your so-called friends deserve what they—"

"No! Mom. You're not listening! I hurt. I hurt so much."

"If I'm hard on you, Natasha," Mom started, "it's because I'm on your side, and I want you to—"

"Ugh! Maybe you could go be on somebody else's side for a little while," I said. "Go be on Truly's side. I need a break."

A small laugh escaped Mom's lips. It seemed like she was trying to hold it in like a burp, but it got away from her.

"What?"

"Nothing. You're funny. You don't even try, and you're . . ." She tossed me my old green sweatshirt from the bed. "You're funny. Did you really step on the glass?"

I nodded, slipping into the comfort of that big sweatshirt. It used to be my dad's. At least there was room for me inside it. She really thinks I'm funny? Funny is good. People like funny. Brooke, especially,

"Let me take a look," Mom said.

"It's okay," I said. "I'm fine."

She patted my bed. I rolled my eyes and sighed. She patted the bed again.

I tiptoed over and sat down next to her. Flipped my legs up onto the comforter and let her look at my huge ruined feet.

"Ooooh," she said. "Stay right here. Don't move. There's a bunch of glass in there. I have to get alcohol, and, I guess, a tweezers, some paper towels, if we have any. Ugh. I think we're out." She picked up the base of the lamp, its shade hanging at an injured angle, and placed it back onto my night table. "I'll find something."

"Can't we just leave bad enough alone?" I asked.

"No," she said, her arms crossed with my dress knotted up around them. "We have to get every last piece out, dodo. Might take some work, and be disgusting, but we can do it. We're tough."

"Do you even know how to do it?"

She turned her face away and sighed. "I'll try," she said. "No promises."

"It's gonna hurt," I said.

She nodded. "It's not gonna be a picnic for me, either." She looked out into the hallway, away from me. "I'll be as gentle as I can. And then we'll see about letting out this dress. Okay?"

"I guess."

"Natasha," she said, turning around.

"What."

"I . . . I'll get some ice," she said. "That might take away some of the pain."

"Okay," I said. "Worth a try."

HAZEL

"SO THAT ANSWERS my first question," I said to Truly when she got to the lockers this morning.

"What question?"

"You're still alive," I said.

She looked at me solemnly. Her hair was shiny and hanging down, no ponytail today, just clipped back on one side. She had on a bit of mascara and no eyeliner, with clear lip gloss. She looked beautiful. Made me almost want to scrub my own face clean. She didn't say anything.

"I'm sorry," I whispered. "As I said in my—you read the e-mails I sent you?"

She nodded.

"I had good reasons but still," I said. "I shouldn't have hacked your accounts."

"No," Truly said. "You shouldn't have."

At least she was talking to me. I held out my hand, open

palm, to give her the lock I had bought her. A word lock. "It spells *friend*," I told her.

She didn't take it.

"You can change the word if you want."

"I'm sorry, too," she said, her head bent. "I know I didn't—"

"No," I said. "You didn't."

We just stood there for a minute, the new lock on my hand like an unchosen hors d'oeuvre. "Maybe keep it as a spare," I suggested after the early bell rang.

She lifted it from my hand.

"I like your bracelet," I said.

Her cheeks pinked up. "Thanks." She turned to her locker and spun her old combination. My plan had been to take her lock off and put the new one on as a surprise, but at the last second I decided against it, as maybe *too much*. She knelt and arranged her things.

"My parents are so upset," she said, toward the inside of her locker.

"They probably hate me," I said.

"They don't." She shook her head. "They just think we all got a little out of hand. They're disappointed that I didn't tell them what was going on with me, and everything."

"Why didn't you?"

"I guess I was trying to not be babyish."

"Oh," I said. "Yeah, but like even my grandmother has people she complains to, tons of them, and she's anything but babyish. She's ancient!"

"She's okay then?"

"She's horrible, but, you know, fine, thanks." It felt so good to talk with Truly again. "My point is, you can be strong and independent but still have backup from people you trust."

"Now you tell me. I'm grounded from going online for a month. They say it's just a cooling down period, take a breather after everything that happened. Not a punishment."

"But that's how it feels?"

"A little," she said. "Yeah."

"As if being online is the problem."

"Right?" She stood up and leaned against the locker beside hers. "Though I guess the online-ness of it did make it all worse."

"And faster and more, like, public."

"Yeah," she agreed. "Exactly."

"I'll ban myself for the month too," I said. "From the whole Internet. Or all screens if you want."

"You don't have to do that."

"I want to," I said. "In solidarity."

She smiled a little. "Okay. Thanks."

"Did you really throw your phone in Big Pond? People were saying."

She nodded. "It's gonna take me until about tenth grade to earn enough to buy a new one."

"I bet," I said.

"Stupid, huh?"

"Nah," I said. "Sometimes a person has to make the grand gesture."

She looked up at me, warmly I think, and said, "Yeah."

"Did it make a glorious splash?"

"Not really, no."

"Well maybe in your memories the splash will grow," I said.

I picked up my triptych presentation on the role of bananas in the rise of the Confederacy. "Did you know bananas played almost no role in the rise of the Confederacy?"

"I hadn't heard."

"Spoiler alert," I said.

She managed a small sympathy smile, then said, "You can go ahead."

"Oh," I said. "Okay." Dismissed.

"Hazel?"

I turned around.

"See you down there," she said. "Okay?"

"Good luck to us all," I said. I picked up my triptych and headed toward the gym, trailing yellow and gold banana glitter behind me.

TRULY

I STOPPED IN the girls' bathroom doorway, halfway in, halfway out. I was planning to take a moment alone before facing them. But no. They were all in there and now it was too late. They'd already seen me.

"Hi," I said. I braced myself. *Whatever they say, I'm okay. I can deal.* That's what my mom told me to remember. *No matter what, I'm okay. Just breathe.*

"Hi, Truly," Brooke said.

I waited. I breathed. I was okay.

"Hey," Brooke went on. "Did you see what happened with all those posts and stuff?"

I shook my head, happy suddenly to have the excuse. "My parents took away my computer for a month."

"Oh," Brooke said. "Sorry. We got most of that crap taken off-line. Some of it we couldn't, but I think we deleted nearly everything mean. About any of us."

"Really?" I asked. "The, all the . . . pictures and, opinions, rumors?"

"Yeah," Brooke said.

"In the trash where it belongs," Evangeline said.

"Well, the virtual trash," Lulu said.

"So you just went through and . . ." *What?* "When?"

"Instead of rehearsing yesterday afternoon," Evangeline said.

"YOLO!" Lulu yelled.

"Yeah, we're gonna bomb today," Natasha said. "We have to use our scripts."

"I'm sure that's fine," I said. "Thanks, you guys. So much."

"Shouldn't have been there to begin with," Brooke said, and shrugged.

"No," I said, looking over at Natasha. "None of it should have."

We both knew she'd been the one who posted at least those pictures of me with kissy faces. She was the only one who had those.

"True," Natasha said. "Whoever posted all that is such a—"

"You look really nice," I interrupted. No need to go there.

"I do?" she asked.

I nodded. I breathed.

"You were right, Natasha," Brooke added. "That dress is perfect."

"And I love the scarf over it," Lulu said. "That's such a great addition. Don't you think, Truly?"

"Yeah," I said.

"How about these sweatpants," asked Evangeline. "Sexy, right?"

"Super hot," Brooke assured her.

Lulu shook a bottle of white hair spray and told Brooke and Evangeline to cover their eyes, then sprayed a toxic cloud onto their hair. It dispersed into the air. Almost invisible, but not quite, and we were all breathing the fumes. A dusting of white covered Brooke's hair and Evangeline's.

"Do I look like George Washington?" Brooke asked, coughing. We all gathered around the sink and looked into the mirror above it, together.

"Totally," Lulu said, and crossed her eyes. "I thought you were a dollar bill, standing there."

"I almost put you in my wallet," I said.

They all laughed. Then Brooke stuck out her tongue at our reflection. Natasha made a fish face. I tilted my head and raised one eyebrow. Evangeline snapped a photo of us in the mirror.

"Let's post that," Brooke said. "We gotta put something good up, right? Not now though. Don't we go first? I think I just forgot everything."

We all grabbed our stuff. As the others rushed out, Natasha grabbed my wrist, the one with the bracelet on it, and held me back.

"Hey," she whispered. "Truly, so you know? I'm not the one who . . ."

"Let's not . . ." I whispered back. "Not right now. Let's just let it all . . . My mom says we should take a break from each other, but . . ."

"Fine." She dropped my hand.

I held the door open and let her walk through. I followed her. "You okay?"

"No, Truly. You killed me. Hurt me to the core. Get over yourself. You want a break? Great, fine, whatever. I actually don't care."

"No," I said. "I meant, you're walking very . . . carefully. Are your feet hurt?"

"Long story," she said. "Don't ask."

"You're always mad at me."

"Yeah," Natasha said. "That's probably true."

"Okay. Well, what I was gonna say is just, instead of talking it through *or* taking a break? Maybe we could just try not to be so mad at each other all the time."

We walked along, side by side, not talking. Both stepping tenderly.

"It's kind of a habit by now," she whispered.

I smiled up at her and nodded. "I know. For me, too. I didn't, I guess I didn't want to know that about myself, but . . ."

"But there it is. Now we know."

"And I'm terrible at breaking habits. Just ask my cuticles." I held out my hands.

"Ew. That is disgusting," she said, slapping them down. "Put that freak show away."

She grabbed the gym door and held it open for me.

"Thanks," I said, and smiled. It wasn't even a fake smile. I don't know fully why.

"Okay," she whispered as I passed through. "I'll try. No promises."

"Fair enough," I whispered back. "Me, too."

Ms. Canuto was under the basketball hoop, yelling into the microphone at everybody to *sit down, settle down! Welcome to History Day please sit!*

Natasha ran on tiptoes to join Brooke, Evangeline, and Lulu in the front corner, beside the flagpole. I sat down at the back, alone.

"No, no, no," Ms. Canuto said into the microphone. "Truly Gonzales! Stand up!"

I stood up. People turned around to look at me.

"You have to introduce the play!" Ms. Canuto said as I stood there, trying not to devour myself fingers first. "Come on up front! Boys and girls, settle down now. For our first event of History Day, we have an original play! Here to introduce the play she wrote—starring Brooke Armstrong, Natasha Lawrence, Lulu Peters, and Evangeline Murphy— is Truly Gonzales! A round of applause and your attention please! Truly? Come up here, dear!"

Great. I walked around the halfheartedly clapping crowd to the front of the gym. As Ms. Canuto lowered the microphone way down to my level, I looked out at the faces of all the kids in the whole eighth grade. They were kind of swimmy, like in my dream of the horrible carnival. There was Hazel, though, watching me. I latched my eyes onto hers like you're supposed to do on the horizon when you're on a boat, to keep from puking out your seasickness.

"This is a play about Benedict Arnold." I gripped the microphone stand. "He was a traitor. A bad guy. As everybody knows."

Toward the back, the guys from the Popular Table sat in a clump. Clay was grinning like it was his birthday. I guess he was psyched for the show. Maybe because Brooke was in it. Or maybe he was just happy to not be in math class. On the edge of that group, Jack held up a small lollipop. I knew what flavor it would be.

"But there's more than one side to the story," I said, smiling at Jack. "There usually is."

I peeked behind me. Lulu was bouncing around. Natasha was fidgeting in her dress while Evangeline clutched the script, muttering the words I'd written. Brooke smiled and gave me a thumbs-up sign.

"The play is called *Benediction*," I said. "Because, well, his name. Benedict. But also *Benediction* because that's what Benedict Arnold wanted most, in the end, a *bene-diction*, which means 'good say.' To be spoken well of. Not riches. Not power, not love, not even to win the war. Just to have people say good stuff about him. Basically, he wanted to be popular. That's all. We didn't invent wanting to be popular, turns out. Hahaha."

Nobody was laughing. I gripped the microphone stand. "So I guess this play is not just a slice of history—it *is* history, don't worry Ms. Canuto, with a bibliography at the end!— But it's also a story about somebody who got so tangled up in wanting people to *think* he was good that he forgot to actually *be* good."

I swallowed hard. Maybe I was saying too much. Not seeming light and easy. Oh, well. I pretty much already fully blew that. "Anyway," I blundered on, "here it is. I hope you like it. Or, whoops, that makes me sound as messed up as Benedict. So, no. Not I hope you like it, even though, honestly? I can't help it. I do hope you like it. Especially you, Ms. Canuto! Well, actually, all of you, really. But more important, I hope it's good. Good in itself. What you guys think about it is ultimately not my business so I'm trying to . . . Ugh. Whatever. Here goes. Thank you."

I went and sat down in the middle of the front row of kids on the cold gym floor. My friends stepped forward for the start of the play. And then it was happening, ready or probably not.